I0689361

Lessons Learned

By Marvin Grayson

Lessons Learned

By: Marvin Grayson

Cover Created & Designed/Images: Leroy Grayson/Quality Pictures

Cover Vision: Marvin Grayson

Interior Images: Photobucket and wfe.smc.edu

Logo Designs: Andre M. Saunders

Editor: Anelda L. Attaway

Co-Editor: Marvin Grayson

© 2016 Marvin Grayson

ISBN 978-0-9970848-4-9

Library of Congress Control Number: 2016961404

ACKNOWLEDGMENTS

First and foremost, I'd like to give thanks to God for giving me the strength to complete this book because without Him I am nothing! Thanks to my grandmothers, Bertha Parker and the late Anna Mae Grayson, Toni Carter, Joyce Cale, Charles Brown, Zelma Blackson, Tina Collins, Tisha Jones, Edward Wilson, Tee Rayfield, Mark Grayson, Tammy Stewart, Dolena Grayson, Leroy Grayson and my publisher Anelda Attaway who has helped me to discover my true voice and put it into text.

A special thank you my family who passed away, Willa Mae Grayson, Ernest Grayson, James Jackson, , Ernest 'Boo' Grayson, Stephon Grayson, Arica Grayson, Kim Grayson, Bernard Grayson, Bertha Church, Joy Carter, LaTanya Scott, Lenny Jackson, Tina Grayson, Eric Grayson, Clyde Grayson, Dana Grayson, and Debbie Grayson. Your memory will never fade. Also, I want to thank all my family and friends not mentioned above.

I look forward to sharing the world as I see it so, take a walk with me through these pages. Everything that I've seen, you shall also see. I hope that you will learn what I've learned and pass it on to the next person because we are never too old to Learn a Lesson. I pray that you find something in this book useful to use in your life to enrich it.

God Bless and Stay Loved and Love Others.

Marvin Grayson

Smile for Me!

DEDICATION

This book is dedicated to all the people who have learned from their mistakes and have grown from them.

TABLE OF CONTENTS

TABLE OF CONTENTS

INTRODUCTION

Bill Freeman, a millionaire who inherits his business from his father who died in a terrible car accident. He meets a young woman named Francine also known as Fran. Bill and Fran will go through numerous changes that will turn both of their lives upside down. They will go through a maze of troubles that will leave them battered and bruised, but will they learn from the problems that life sometimes throws at them or will they let it destroy them?

Fran gives birth to a son who will grow up and find out that life is not always peaches and cream and will struggle with his own devices. As betrayal and deceit become commonplace where Only the Strong Will Survive. Those who use treachery as a guide and will fall victim to their own weapons.

Read as people will learn in the largest classroom ever created, the human mind where many will fail because of lack of knowledge and the will to survive. Or will they want to live and fight another day? He or she who uses people for financial or sexual gain will have their reward because everything they gain will not be good and will fall by their own devices. If you are a person who uses deception as a guide, it will lead nowhere. Treat people like you would like to be treated and all that is good will be added to you, but if you live life as a spider you will eventually fall victim to your own Web of Lies, Greed, Deceit, and Betrayal. I would like to also share this, those people who mix jealousy and lust together are flirting with danger because it is a recipe for death. Therefore, don't use people to gain anything because after you get it you will find it wasn't worth it. If you like using people, in the end, you'll be the only one being used.

LESSON 1

Always Look Both Ways
Before Crossing the Street of Life

It was a cold night, December 22, 1960. Bill Freeman was sitting at Sam's Café on 42nd Street in New York City he was young and full of life.

His grandfather started a company called Dark Water Oils in 1931. Bill's father Robert passed away last year in a car accident and it was a very tough time for him. It hurt him so much that sometimes he would not eat for days. His father was the best thing in his life. Robert Freeman was more than a father, he was his best friend. He told Bill that if he wanted to make it in this world, he had to get what he wanted himself and not ask anybody for anything. But Bill wanted to do things his way, he was a rich kid with rich parents, they had a lot of money. Bill's mother died giving birth so, he never knew her, only through pictures. The company his grandfather started was worth well over 500 million dollars with refineries all over the world. He lived the lavish life, but with his father and mother gone, none of that meant anything to him. Also, he struggled with the fact that his father was no longer around to tell him when he was screwing up. He had to find out what life was all about himself.

Bill often gave his father a hard time when it came to taking advice, which he did not do very well. Sometimes he would take his father's car and go out partying with his friends, and not come back for days. He would go out spending hundreds of dollars on prostitutes without fear from his father. One time, he met a girl who claimed someone robbed her and she had no money to feed her kids. Therefore, she asked if could he help her.

As he went to pull his wallet out to give her $20 she pulled a gun and said, "You give me the wallet, you keep the 20."

He said, "You must be joking."

She asked, "Do I look like I'm playing? Hand, it over before I shoot your Ass."

Bill gave her his wallet and kept the $20. Then she ran to jump in someone's car. They pulled off as she yelled out the window, "Don't spend that 20 dollars in one place!"

Bill often thought of what could he do to get over losing his father and at that moment she walked in. *She was an angel, he thought to himself that has come down from Heaven to save him from himself.* She proceeded to walk by his table, he grabbed her hand and asked her, "Are you looking for me?"

And she quickly responded, "I don't know you, but will you get to know me for my heart is broken. I look for you to free me from my pain."

The girl's name was Fran Smith; she was coming into work at Sam's Café as a waitress. Fran was 18 years old, her father was a construction worker, who got drunk and beat the living crap out of her and her mother often. Fran wanted to kill her father, but could never get up the nerve. Fran's mother did not work; however, she was a good housewife and she took care of her family. But her husband gave her Hell on Earth.

He introduced himself, "I'm Bill and your Fran."

"How do you know my name?" she asked.

"Your name tag," he responded.

"Oh?" she quickly responded."

And then he asked, "Fran will you marry me? I will take care of you for the rest of your life and you will never have to work gain."

She asked, "Are you Bullshit'n me?"

And Bill replied, "I love you already and I don't even know you."

Fran said, "Yes, I'll marry you; is this Candid Camera?"

"No," Bill said, "I want to tell you something, I don't like blonde hair, you're going to have to change it. Will you change it?"

"Let me tell you something about me. I don't like Assholes so please don't be one. I will not change my hair! I happen to like my hair and if you don't like it you can Fuck Off!"

Bill said, "I guess I can get used to your blonde hair."

"And I guess I can get use to you being an Asshole. Let's go get married, that settles that."

It was 7 o'clock when Fran got home, her mother was in the kitchen cooking dinner and her father was on the sofa drunk in front of the TV like he is every night.

Fran steps in the door and starts to speak, "I have good news."

And her father said, "What you got a facelift? You ugly Bitch."

Fran responded, "You don't talk to me like that you Piece of Shit and like I said Mom I have good news."

"What is it Dear?"

"I'm getting married."

"To who?" her father asked, "he must be blind to marry your ugly Ass."

Her father always called her ugly when he started drinking and out of the clear blue he said, "Where's my dinner woman?"

"I can't get dinner on time and this dumb whore comes in here telling us she's getting married."

Then he asked, "How long have you known this fella?"

Fran answers, "I just met him today."

Her mother then asked, "Have you lost your mind? You don't even know this fella."

And her father said scrasitically, "How can this dumb girl lose something she never had?"

Her mother quickly responds, "You can't be serious Honey."

Fran said, "I am and he is very rich. And he told me I was an Angel and if I marry him I would never have to work again."

Her father replied, "You believe that Crap? You're even dumber than I thought you were; you will work always even if it's on your back; you Cheap Whore!"

"I'm tired of your Shit," she said and picks up a lamp that she was standing by and throws it at her father. It strikes him right in the head.

He starts cursing and yells to his wife, "Call the cops! I want this girl locked up and you better call them or I'm going to take the same lamp and go upside your head with it."

Then Fran tells her mother, "After you call for him, tell the police someone else would like to speak with them concerning another matter. I'm sure they'll love to hear what I have to say."

Then her father asked, "Can't we all just get along? There's no need for the police; we can take care of my own problems."

Then Fran said, "I knew you would see it my way."

Her father is sitting down holding a cloth over his head and said to Fran, "I'm sorry for talking to you the way I did. I will never do that again, and you know why? Because you won't be here. I want you out of my house, like right now."

Fran said, "Fine!" And goes to her room to get her things.

She is very upset with him and said, "I'm going to the police for what you did to me. I'm leaving, but this is not over!"

Fran's mother is crying, "I want my Baby to stay here. She's only 18-years-old."

He replied, "I don't care, I want her gone."

Then Fran goes over to her father and slaps him hard in the face and then said, "That's for making my life a Living Hell!" And walks out the door saying, "chew on that you Old Fart!"

Fran starts walking down the road toward a phone booth to call Bill. It was about 10 o'clock when Fran finally called him. *She took about 2 hours to clear her head and wondered was this one big joke and was she at the Ass end of it. She also thought about her father and how she would make him pay for what he did to her and her mother all those years.* She felt sorry for her mother and started to cry because she was there alone with that monster. But once she married into money, she would be able to take her mother away from all that pain. She is a very sweet kind women who is being taken advantage of by that drunk. *Fran thought to herself, "I will fix his wagon so he won't be able to hurt us anymore."*

She walked slowly dragging her feet while carrying her bags down that long road from her mother's trailer. Someone pulled over to give her a ride. She looked in to see who was driving. It was Old Man Blue who lives down from her former home.

He stops and asked, "Can I give you a lift Little Lady?"

She answered, "How far are you going?"

He replied, "I'm going into town."

"That's great! That's where I'm headed."

He replied, "Alright then, get in."

She gets in the car and sits back. Old Man Blue is looking at Fran with lust in his eyes.

She asked, "What are you staring at you Old Geezer? Just drive and keep your eyes on the road before you hit something."

Old Man Blue tells her she is a pretty girl and she shouldn't be walking alone because someone might try to take advantage of her.

She said to him, "You would be the first one to try."

He replied, "I wouldn't do a thing like that unless you gave me permission."

"I don't have to worry about you then because you will never get it," she said.

Old Man Blue arrived at the shopping store. Fran starts to get out of the car and Old Man Blue is staring again, but this time he grabs her breast. She gets out of the car and yells, "You Old Pervert! If you ever touch me like that I'm going to snatch your dentures out of your mouth and beat you over the head with them! You got that!?" Then she walks away.

Fran finally finds a phone booth and calls Bill. The phone rang two times and then Bill answered.

"Hello is Bill there?"

"Speaking."

Fran said, "It's me calling."

He replied, "Who's me? I don't know anybody by that name."

She quickly said, "I met you this morning at Sam's Café."

"I'm sorry Miss, I don't know any 'Me', you must have the wrong number." She was shocked, her jaw dropped and then she heard a click. Bill hung up on her.

"Oh, My God, I'm on the street and out of my house, my parents think I'm crazy. I don't know what I'm going to do," she thought to herself. And then the phone rang.

She became excited, picked up the receiver and said, "Hello."

The voice on the other end asked, "Is Fran there?"

"Speaking…Bill is that you?" she replied."

"It's me, My Love," he said.

"You almost gave me a heart attack you Asshole."

"Sorry Honey, I got to keep you on your toes."

Fran replied, "If you ever scare me like that again my toes and my whole foot are going to be Stuck in your Ass!"

"I want to say that I could not keep my mind off you, I thought of you all the time when you were gone," he said.

"I thought about you also and how you would come get me, your Queen and take me to your castle far away."

"I was thinking the same thing; tell me where you are and I will come pick you up soon as I can."

"I'm on Memory Lane right next to Carmen's Hair Salon," she said.

He replied, "I will be there in 20 minutes."

"I'm going to count the seconds, so hurry it's cold.".

"I will see you in a few shakes," he said.

Fran felt a lot better after talking to Bill. He was on his way to pick her up and she will be on her way to a new life.

LESSON 2

Time Waits for No Man or Woman

Bill arrived an hour later; Fran was not feeling too good about Bill being late.

"I thought you said you would be here in 20 minutes?" Fran asked Bill.

"It was a car accident on the highway; traffic was backed up for miles, that's why I'm late," he answered.

"Well, at least you showed up and didn't leave me hanging," she said.

"Just get in the car Blondie," he said quickly.

She gets in the car and said, "This is a nice car." It was a Mercedes Benz.

Then she asked Bill, "Can I have one like this? But not this color, maybe Candy Apple Red."

"If you play your cards right, there will be nothing that you can't have," Bill replied.

"I play cards pretty well. I plan on winning at any game," she said as she kissed Bill on the nose.

"What's wrong with my lips?"

"I don't know you like that, besides your breath stinks."

Bill replies, "Does it really?"

Then Fran cuts him off and said, "It smells like Shit! Whose toilet have you been playing in, you naughty Boy?" Then she continues saying, "don't worry, I have emergency gum." Then hands Bill the gum.

Bill replied, "What's that?"

"It's when you stick gum or mint in your mouth with the wrapper still on because there's no time to take it off because you can hurt somebody with that thing," she said with urgency. Bill and Fran both laughed all the way to Bill's house about his foul breath.

Bill and Fran arrived at his house around midnight. His house was in the suburbs of West Overhills where houses cost well over 1 million dollars. Bill had a big house, but it did not look like it cost a million dollars, but it was nice.

"I can get used to this kind of living. Do we have a maid?" Fran asked.

"Yes, we do," he answered with his eyebrows raised.

"What's with the eyes?" Fran asked, "what are you…messing with the help?"

"No, I don't see her like that."

She replied, "You like to see her with her clothes off. Don't you?"

"She comes once a week."

"That's all? We need her all week because I don't want to lift a finger. Especially, if I don't have to. Besides, I don't cook that well. I will cook dinner sometimes if you don't mind burnt food," Fran said.

"I like my food cooked well done, but not that done. Never mind that stuff about food. I want to know about your family?" he asked.

"I don't have much to say, I'm a little White girl from a trailer park who has been poor all her life, and grew up too fast. My father's name is Jim and he drinks too much. My mother's name is Jane and she is the sweetest mom a person can have. Enough about me tell me, how you got to be so rich?"

"Well it's a long story; anyway, my grandfather started a company called Dark Water Oils. One day he was digging in the ground for water and he struck oil, Black Gold, Texas Tea, just like those hillbillies and he started selling oil and my family has been rich ever since."

"How are your parents doing?" she asked.

"Both of my folks are dead. My mother died giving birth; I didn't know her, but I miss her. I just lost my father; he passed away last year, and I miss him very much. I never heard him because I knew it all until the day I got that call and he was no longer there. I wanted to tell him I was sorry for being an Ass Bucket, but I can't and it tears me apart every day. But I'm getting better; I don't like to talk about my father because it's too painful. I would love to talk about something that does not make my eyes water," he said.

She touched his shoulder and for a moment, Fran felt something for this man that she did not know. The day came when Bill and Fran got married. They had disagreements the entire time they were living together. It was a simple wedding. Bill paid $3000 for a gown for his wife to be and she looked ravishing. *Bill thought to himself, "I can't wait to make love to her on our honeymoon."*

"I want to take you to Paris," he said to her.

"And we will share moments that will live forever and I will enjoy every second," Fran said, "I want you to promise you'll be gentle with me."

"What are you a virgin?"

"Yes," she answered, "it will be my first time."

Bill smiled and said, "This will truly be special."

"Yes, it will my Sweet Friend," she replied.

Bill and Fran left for the airport; he had his private jet waiting so they could leave quickly. It took 7½ hours to get there; they arrived 2am in France. They checked in at a hotel and enjoyed a quiet dinner by candlelight.

Bill said to her, "You are a bride that Heaven sent and for that reason, I shall love you always, no matter what we go through I will be at your side."

Fran said, "Please stop you're going to make me cry."

"Let your feelings out, if you must cry do so because I know they will be tears of joy," Bill replied.

"I will order now," Fran said to the waiter.

"What will you be having Miss?" the waiter asked.

"I would like to order your roast duck in wine sauce and a light salad, please."

"Very well, will you be ordering too Sir?" the waiter asked Bill.

"Yes, I have your stuffed clams with lobster and a bottle of your best wine."

Bill and Fran ate their dinner and talked about the future and children while listening to soft music in the background.

"I would like to have this dance with you, My Love."

"Why not? You bought these shoes, this dress and I wouldn't want you to feel cheated. You're the man I want to dance with forever and hold you close to my heart. Ooooh, I feel your manhood on my leg."

"I'm sorry Dear, but you're so desirable I can't wait to make love to you."

"And you will soon enough," she said.

Bill and Fran danced for hours just holding each other close like it was their last day on earth. Then Bill told Fran that he would never love another as long as she is alive.

And Fran replied, "That's good to know because you won't be loving anybody else for a long time. I plan on being around."

"I hope so because I don't know what I would do without your smile," he said.

And Fran replied, "I feel the same way because I don't know what I would do without your money."

He quickly said to her, "I don't know what I would do without my money either; I have lived with money all of my life. So, if I lost it, I would find the highest building and jump off."

"I hope that doesn't happen because I need the freedom your money will give me. All this talk of money, suicide and dying is putting me in the mood," she said.

Then Bill said smiling while grabbing Fran's hand, "I was in Love when I first saw you."

Bill finished the bottle of wine. Fran had two glasses and she was slightly drunk.

She looked at Bill and said, "Our bed awaits." They got up and went to their room that cost over $2000 a night. They entered the room and they immediately noticed a bottle of champagne with two glasses on the bar. Bill asked Fran if she wanted another drink to take the edge off before they retire into the bedroom. She said yes and walked by Bill grabbing the bottle out of his hand and walked into the room.

Bill said, "Come back here, let's do this right."

"Do what right?" she said. "I have to carry you into the room, so let's walk back to the door and start over."

"Alright let's do it," she said.

Bill carried Fran into the room and dropped her on the bed. She bounced off it and landed onto the floor. Bill laughed so hard he forgot to help her up. But after he got himself together he helped her up off the floor.

"Are you alright?" he asked."

"I'm fine, but I don't know about my back."

At that moment, he looked into her eyes and kissed her gently on her lips and she gasps as her gown hit the floor. Bill stepped back to admire this beauty. He looked at her body and ripped his clothes off; buttons popping and zippers snapping, shirt tearing and shoes flying without saying a word.

Fran said, "You don't waste any time, do you? Don't rush we have all night because if we rush we might miss something and I don't want to miss anything on my special night."

Bill said, "You're right Honey, I will have to slow down."

"Please do," she said.

Bill gently embraced Fran and started kissing her softly on her lips. Fran began to feel the heat within her body. Bill lowered her down on the bed, and she opened her legs to receive him.

He said, "I will be gentle with you since this is your first time."

He entered her expecting to get a little tightness since she said she was she was a virgin. However, he slid right inside her with ease. *Therefore, he thought to himself, "She's no virgin."* But it felt so good therefore he said nothing while thrusting in and out. And he kissed her while rubbing her perky breasts. She screamed with delight as they made love. They both came to an Earth-Shaking Climax. Then Bill got up and sat on the side of the bed, not saying anything.

"What's wrong with you?" Fran asked.

"You know what's wrong with me, you lied to me. You told me you were a virgin," he replied.

"I don't know what to say," she said, "I didn't mean to lie to you, but it was something that I couldn't talk about. Besides, I didn't think you would notice with your Little Dick."

Bill felt a little hurt with Fran's statement. She cut Bill's knees off with the words she used because he had a dumb look on his face.

"You did not have to go there," he said.

"Yeah, but I went there," she said, "all you had to do was come in here and stick your little Thing in and enjoy yourself, but instead you had to open your stupid mouth complaining about my sex. You loved it."

"I thought you should have told me," Bill said.

"Told you what? That my father molested me since I was 8-years-old? Well, I don't like to think about it because it hurts too bad; smelling his breath after he has been drinking and him inside of me. You satisfied now? You had to ruin my wedding night with some Bullshit that don't matter."

"I'm sorry," Bill said, "I should have kept that to myself."

"You sure should have because now I'm going to keep my Pussy to myself since it's not tight enough for you. I bet you can adjust your hand to fit just right," she said and turned over and went to sleep.

Bill felt like a real Jackass, as he sat on the edge of the bed looking at his wife's Naked Ass while thinking that he should masturbate, but he decided not to and went to sleep.

The morning came and Fran and Bill got up early since they did not do too much to make them sleep late. They ate breakfast, but Fran wasn't that hungry. All she ate was a fruit salad and drank a cup of coffee. Bill, on the other hand, ate a full course meal. *He was thinking to himself, "What have I got myself into?"* He felt like he jumped out of the frying pan into a pot of sizzling grease, but was determined to ride it out.

"I would like to do some shopping today Honey and some sightseeing," Fran said.

"That will be fine, I always wanted to see France in the Spring and ride in those funny looking cars," he replied.

"I'm going to get dressed," she said and proceed to the bedroom.

And Bill was right behind her hoping she would give him sex before they left. Fran took her housecoat off to take a shower. And once again Bill was behind her.

Therefore, she asked him, "Where are you going?"

He quickly replied, "To take a shower with you."

"Oh, no you're not! You'll wait until I'm done and then you can take one, besides I'm not having sex. I'm not in the mood, you spoiled that last night."

"Now how long are you going to hold that against me?" Bill asked.

"As long as I want. And don't ask me for sex, I will let you know when I'm ready. Got that Sweetie Pie?"

"Sure," he said in a low voice, but he did not like it.

Bill felt less than a man allowing his woman to talk to him this way. Fran knew that the more she talked mean belittling him, the powerless he became and the more powerful she became.

Fran and Bill both took their showers and went out for the day. They had a good time. Fran spent $7,000 on clothes and shoes, Bill brought a few things and they stayed in France for two days before going back to the States.

When they returned, Fran did not know she was pregnant and that in 9 months she would have a little baby. Well, two babies because she treats

Bill like a kid. He hated the way she treated him, but he got himself in this mess and he will get himself out of it, so he thought. But Fran had plans. One of her plans was to teach him that you don't marry a person the first time you meet them because that person is a stranger and may be a wolf in sheep's clothing.

LESSON 3

The Eyes Are the Window to the Soul

The fact that Fran carried Tony for 9 months, Bill was very happy. He was happy because he was about to be a father and it's going to be a boy. Fran was just as happy as Bill and maybe more because she was about to become a part of life that makes life worth living. Bill had to put up with Fran's eating habits. And on one occasion she woke him up in the middle of the night to go to the supermarket to get a Snickers bar and a pickle.

Bill was real upset about that and he told her, "Fran I know you're pregnant, but you have to pick some better times to ask me to go someplace, and not ask me when I'm trying to get some Fucking sleep."

Fran replied, "I will ask you what I want and when I want and if you don't do what I ask I will cut your Little Dick off and shove it up your White Ass. Don't play with me I'm not your child."

Bill looked at Fran with a cold stare, thinking to himself, "What have I done? This Fucking Bitch is crazy." Then he tells her, "I don't have a problem doing what you asked me, just ask me when I'm not doing something I like and it's called sleeping!"

"You must not have heard what I told you before, I will ask you for what I want and when I want. I might not cut your Dick off, but I may want you to give me a little something sometimes. But I will go upside your head with one of those frying pans in the kitchen."

"I'm not getting into a war of words with you Fran," Bill said.

"Then don't," she replied, "I said what I had to say and try me and see what you get. I don't know why I married you in the first place; you're an

Asshole!" she said, "oh yes, I do, know why I married you, you got the money Honey, and if you ever try to leave me I will take you for everything you own. How about that?"

It's April 3, 1964, Fran and Bill have been going through a lot. Bill feels like he's walking on eggshells with this woman because she won't give him a break. Bill felt bored one day and decided to do a little yard work so he went to the shed to get some tools to fix the lawn mower. The lawn mower has been broken for a long time and he felt he could fix it.

Fran is also bored, so she decided to do the laundry and she yells to Bill, "I'm out of bleach, can you ride to the store to get some!"

He yells back, "I will go when I'm done here!"

I guess he forgot who he was dealing with. However, Bill proceeded to fix the lawn mower not realizing that Fran is fast approaching. Bill felt someone behind him and Fran flashed before his eyes. After that, he heard and felt the frying pan against his head.

The next thing Bill knew, he was being revived with a water hose and as soon as he came to he asked, "What happened?"

Fran, it's looking down on him with the water flowing all over his face and she replied, "I told you what I would do if you did not do what I asked you."

"But you did not give me a chance, I was going to take care of it," he said.

"Well, I felt that you didn't move fast enough and that's why you find yourself down there wondering what happened."

"Can you help me up?" he asked.

"No," she replied, "help yourself."

"You are one crazy lady and I see that you carried your plans out with the frying pan thing. And you did it because you know I don't hit women, but if you keep pushing me I might change that and beat you with that Damn flying pan. So, keep your hands to yourself!" he yelled.

"I hear you, but all I'm saying is if you Piss me off on the wrong day, I'll crack the other side of your head. How do you like that? Also, if you put your Dick Beaters on me, I will put you under the jail."

Immediately Bill starts rubbing his head and thinks to himself, "I'm in trouble." Bill wanted to hit Fran whenever she hit him, but he could not do it because he knew she would call the police on him and have him locked up. Also, he did not want his name in the newspapers or something. Besides, he had a reputation to protect. Therefore, he would let his wife beat him up to keep it.

Fran always started with Bill, it was as if she wanted him to hit her. He figured that Fran missed her father beating her up so, she took it out on him and that she is a very mixed up young lady. But never the less, he still wants to help her, if he doesn't kill her first.

Fran started to become a thorn in Bill's side, but he loved her. But the question is, did she love him? Fran was taking Bill through it. For example, anytime Bill wanted to go out by himself she would take his clothes that were pressed and ready to wear and throw them in the shower with him.

LESSON 4

Honor Thy Father and Thy Mother
And Your Days Will be Long Upon the Earth

The date was April 29, 1965, when Fran gave birth to a 6-ounce baby boy that she named Tony. Tony had eyes like his father and a nose like his mother. He grew up fast telling his father at 3-years-old to kiss his Ass because he heard his mother say it to his father so many times. The fact is, he was truly a little brat who needed a spanking every time he opened his mouth. But his mother, on the other hand, thought it was funny the way he behaved sometimes. Until one day he was playing with matches and set her hair on fire while she was asleep.

And she woke up yelling, "Something is burning!"

And then she turned to find her 6-year-old son laughing. At that moment, she felt the heat and realized it was her who was burning. She took off running to the nearest sink to put the fire out. She was so mad at Tony that she beat him with whatever she could find. He cried until he saw the back of her head because she had a big bald spot where he started the fire. He was laughing and crying at the same time.

Fran said to him, "You little Fucker," and threw a glass vase at him. Fortunately, the vase did not hit Tony, instead, it hit the wall. But Tony mouth was so smart and he said, "Nah! Na! Na! Nah! You missed!" And then he ran outside.

She picked up the broken glass on the floor and went to fix her hair. What was left of it anyway? She looked in the mirror and laughed to herself because she knew he was just like her and he was going to give her hell. She would see how he was mean most of the time, but acted like an Angel when he wanted something.

Bill had a house built in the backyard for Tony to play in. It had real running water and a little car garage. It was the real thing, but smaller. Tony even had a small car to fit in the garage. Tony had things other kids only dreamed about. Bill had lots of money and Tony could get his father to buy him anything he wanted. Fran would also get anything she wanted. In fact, she wouldn't waste any time, she would spend thousands of dollars each time she went shopping. Bill told her she was going to break him with her suspending. He also told her she should get off her Lazy Ass and get a job.

So, she quickly replied, "A job? You told me I would never have to work."

"I must have been out of my mind," Bill said, "I think you are a little crazy in your head."

Fran said, "Why do you say that? Maybe you're the one crazy because you married me and you did not know if I was an ax murderer, a drug dealer or crazy Bitch. And guess what, you're stuck with me.

LESSON 5

Never Let your Left-Hand Know
What your Right-Hand is Doing

The years has passed by, it was time for Tony to start middle school and he looked forward to it. Bill and Fran didn't beat Tony so, he thought he should get his way all the time. Although Tony was tough, one day maybe he would meet someone who would kick his Ass and he would find out that he was not as tough as he thought he was.

Tony said to his mother Fran, "If anybody gives me any stuff I will kick their Ass."

"Watch your mouth," his mother said.

"Sorry, I meant someone's Butt."

"I hope you get yourself a girlfriend," his mother said, "then maybe you will stop choking your Chicken."

Bill immediately jumped into the conversation and said, "Leave the boy alone Fran, he can choke his Chicken all he wants. Besides all boys do that growing up."

"So, I guess you're still growing up also because you do that a lot and you can blame your big mouth for that," she said.

"I'm not going there with you," Bill replied.

"And you won't until I want you to, until then Choke On."

Bill decided not to reply to her and skipped the conversation. Instead, he asked Tony, "Did you pick your classes yet?"

"No sir," Tony answered.

"Well you need to pick them; also, I don't want you hanging out with the wrong crowd," Bill said.

"I won't just don't pick my friends for me, I will pick my own. Because I know you two don't like people, especially Black people. And I don't care about a person's color just as long as they are not Assholes, we can get along just fine. Because I will put my foot in White Person's Ass as well as a Black Person's Ass," said. Tony.

"Watch your dirty mouth," his mother said.

"Sorry mom I can't help it; Asshole, Fuck, Shit, and Dick Wipe, are words that are a part of me."

Fran quickly responded, "Tony if you use any more foul words in front of me I'm going to kick your Ass."

Tony said, "See what I mean."

"Don't play with me!" she yelled.

"Okay," Tony replied.

The next day Tony attended school. But the following week Bill wanted Tony to go to a private school, but he did not want to go.

Therefore, he said, "Private school is for boys that are Faggots. And I want to go where the action is. Besides, I don't like those uniforms and make me look funny."

However, he would continue going to the inner city public school. The school he went to was mostly Blacks and a few Whites. Because he went to a public-school Bill rewarded him anyway.

Bill brought Tony a car for his birthday and he wanted to drive it to school. Fran told him to forget about it because he was too young to drive. But sometimes he would take it anyway. Tony could drive pretty well because his father taught him. One day Tony took the car when his mother left early to go somewhere and he did this a lot. And one day on the way to school Tony hit the back of this woman's car. After the wreck, he got out and the lady got out.

She asked him, "Whose car have you stolen?"

He replied, "It's mine."

"I'm calling the police!" she cried.

"Okay but first can I get something out of the car?" he asked. Tony opened the door and quickly jumped in the car and pulled off.

The lady yelled, "Come back here!" But he was gone. Nevertheless, before he pulled off she got his tag number.

Tony went on to school and he parked two blocks from it so no one would see him. Therefore, after school, he could sneak back home and park the car. Fran started taking Tony to school after his little fender bender. He started making friends fast and was well liked by his classmates. He did not want his friends to know that he was a rich brat because they would treat him differently and they would only be his friend because of it.

The one class he took and liked was Gym because he did not have to write anything. He also made a new friend there, his name was Danny. He was from the Lower East Side of New York. He lives with his mother who was 6-months pregnant with her third child and his little sister. Danny was the oldest. He was White and had a hard time when he first came to Canon Middle School. The other students would make fun of him because he wore the same clothes for more than 3 days, but he was clean. His mother washed his stuff every night. He would get very upset when they teased him, but he wouldn't say anything. Until one day a kid named James attempted to take his lunch money.

He walked up to Danny and said, "Give me all your lunch money or I will beat your Ass."

"Danny said, "I'm giving you nothing because I don't have anything." James went to grab him and Danny kicked him in the Nuts. James fell to the floor in pain.

"I'm going to get you for this!" he cried.

"I don't care; I'm not scared of you; I won't let you push me around anymore Shit Head!"

Tony was happy to see Danny stick up for himself. They became best friends after that. Tony wanted Danny to meet his parents. And because he talked about him all the time, they wanted to meet him too. Tony even told his folks how he and Danny played pranks on people at school. Like the time, they switched someone's shampoo with hair removal and when they took a shower all their hair fell out. Tony and Danny cracked up as they told them. That was one of many jokes they played. He also told them about how they were both scared of girls, but they will talk when spoken to. It was one girl that Tony liked, her name was Jennifer Parker. She was 14-years-old, which was one year older than Tony. Jennifer was a pretty young White female who was a cheerleader, a part of the Chess Club and ran the Student Newspaper. He wanted to say something to her, but he could not get up the nerve.

One day Tony spotted Jennifer, so he walked toward her hoping she would say something to him, but she did not. Therefore, he walked right into her on purpose.

"Oh, I'm sorry," he said because he had knocked her books out of her hands.

"Watch where you're walking Shorty," Jennifer said.

"I'm not that short, just low to the ground," he said back to her.

"You're still short," she replied.

"I have not told you my name," Tony said.

Jennifer replied, "I may not want it."

"I already know yours," he said.

"What is it?" she asked.

"It's Jen, short for Jennifer," he said.

"Well, I guess I'm glad to meet you since you went through all this trouble to meet me. I can't understand how you ended up on this side of the hall when you were over there," she said.

"I had to get your attention," he said.

"I know you could have picked a better way to introduce yourself, like asking me what my name was Shorty," she said.

"Stop calling me that, my name is Tony," he replied.

"Okay I'm sorry, but me being a little taller, I can't help it," she said, "and I have to look down on you, but we can still be friends."

"I would love to be your friend because I have never had a friend pretty as you," he said, "I have to go now, it was nice meeting you. I'll see you around."

"Okay," she said.

Tony replied, "How about lunch?"

"Sure," she answered.

Tony's mom came to pick him up at 3 o'clock. Tony and Danny were waiting in front of the school and they were talking about Jennifer.

When Tony's mother pulled up he yelled, "Hey Mom, can you give Danny a ride home!?"

"Where do you live?" she asked.

"By Tommy's Barbershop."

"Where's that?" she asked with a funny grin on her face, "tell me how to get there. And I don't have all day to play around with you two."

"It's about 10 blocks from here," Danny said. When they arrived at Danny's house his mother was waiting on the porch.

"I'm going to kick your Ass Boy!" she yelled.

"For what?" he asked.

"For leaving the stove on and nearly burning down this house!"

When Danny reached the porch, his mother smacked him in the back of his head and told him to get in there and wash that pan out. Danny's mother waved as she pushed him into the house and said thanks.

LESSON 6

What You Do in the Dark
Will Come to the Light

Fran had not talked to her mother since she left those many years ago, but she would write and send her money. And if she tried to call her father would not let her talk. Because most of the time he would just hang up if he knew it was Fran. However, Fran loved her mother and wanted her to come live with her and Bill. But her mother told Fran her father needed her.

Fran snapped, "He treats you like Shit and beats you whenever he feels like it. How long do you want to live like that?"

"But he still loves me," she said.

"You call that love Fran," responded.

"He's not that bad," her mother replied.

"Are you crazy? He has you brainwashed, thinking what he does to you is alright. One day he's going to kill you if you stay," said Fran.

"It's not going to get that bad," her mother said.

"I hope not for your sake. Mom, there's something I've been wanting to talk to you about."

"About what Dear," her mom said.

"Remember I told Daddy he was going to pay for what he did to me and what he is doing to you now.? Well, I'm going to the police for what he did those many years ago, Mom you knew what he was doing to me and you stood by and did nothing!"

"But he said if I told anyone he would kill me and you," her mother said as she started to cry, "I'm sorry but I did not want you to get hurt."

"I was hurt and I'm still hurting to this day I carry that Shit he did to me every day of my life thanks to you," she replied.

"I'm very sorry," her mother said, "what do you want me to do?"

"I want you to pack your stuff and move with me before that drunk does something crazy."

"I can't leave right now," she said.

"Why not?" Fran asked.

"Because he needs me."

"Alright Mom, stay there if you want, but I'm calling the police to help you get out of there as soon as I get done talking to you."

Fran heard a voice in the background, "Are you talking to the Bitch?" her father asked drunk.

"No, I'm talking to Elaine," she said.

"I hope so because you better not be talking to that Rich Whore!" he yelled.

Fran hears him and quickly responded, "Look, Mom, I'll call you back later after I talk to the police."

"Okay he's coming...bye Dear," she said and then hangs up.

Fran arrived at the police station around 10am.

She was sitting alone waiting on Officer Gary Smit, who walks out and said, "You must be Miss Fran Freeman."

"I am."

"What can I do for you, Sweet Thing?"

"My name is not Sweet Thing, it's Fran in case you forgot; I'm here to press charges on someone," she said.

"And who is this someone?" the office asked.

"My father," she said.

"And what are the charges?"

"Rape," she answered.

"When did this happen?" he asked.

"When I was 8-years-old up until 16," she answered.

"And how old are you now?" the officer asked.

"22."

"I would like you to sign some paperwork, then we will send someone out to pick him up," the officer said to Fran.

"I want my father to pay for what he did to me and my mother."

The officer said, "I will be right back with the paperwork so the wheels of justice can turn on that Creep."

"I hope so because he needs to pay for his crime, there is no telling how many people he has done this to," Fran said, "I remember when I was younger, a girl who lives across the road from me was raped and they never found out who done it, and the same night my father had scratches all over his neck. I think he is the one that done it so, he needs to be put away for a long time." It happened so fast when the police arrived. They knocked on the door and Fran's mother answered.

"Is Jim Smith here?" the officer asked.

"Yes," she replied.

"We have an arrest warrant," one of the officers said.

"For what?"

"Rape," the police officer said.

"He did not do it," she said as she blocked the door that led to the room that her husband was in.

"Please get out of the way ma'am and let us do our job before we lock you up."

Then quickly the officer walked in with 3 other officers. Jim stood up to greet them and asked, "What's this about?"

"You are accused of Rape," the officer said.

"By who?" he asked.

"Your daughter."

"Mr. Smith, you have the Right to remain Silent, anything you Say can and will be held against you in a Court of Law. If you don't have an attorney, one will be appointed to you. Do you understand? Stand up Sir," the officer said.

Jim stood up and he was handcuffed while yelling, "I didn't do anything! She let me have sex with her, it was Consensual! She wanted it! I can't help she is a Little Whore." The officer quickly grabbed him around his neck choking him with one hand telling him to shut up.

Jim began to spit and gag yelling, "I got rights!"

The officer said, "You don't have anything, you Fucking Pervert!"

Then he was dragged by the officers to the car fighting and kicking and was thrown in the back seat. He sat there in a trance and then came to the realization that he may spend the rest of his life in prison.

Jim was booked and fingerprinted. Soon he appeared in front of a judge who gave him $20,000 bail. And while in the holding cell he asked the turnkey officer, "Can I get one phone call?"

"No, we don't give phone calls to Child Molesters," he said.

One of the men in the other cell heard the officer and Jim talking and said, "We have a Baby Rapist in our mists."

Jim heard the other inmates and immediately became very nervous and scared.

Another inmate said, "So you like messing with little girls Old Man? I hope they put you in my cell when we get to Lock up. Because I'm going to turn you into a Faggot, Old Man."

The thought of someone Fucking him in his Shitbox sent shivers up his spine and he began to yell, "I need a phone call!"

The turnkey officer came to his cell and opened it and said, "Three minutes on the phone."

As Jim walked by the cells the inmates spit all in his face. By the time, he got to the phone he was covered in spit. The officer gave him a paper towel to wipe it off. He called his wife and told her what his bail was and to come down and get him out. She told him that she would go to the courthouse and pay the bail. He was released 3 hours later and his wife was waiting in the car. So, he walked to the car door and opened it, got in and told her to pull off with urgency in his voice. So, she did as he asked. His wife looked at him perplexed and confused and did not know what to say to a man whose mind fringes on the edge of madness. Jim then told his wife to stop at a liquor store to buy something to drink.

Therefore, his wife pulled into a parking lot of the store and then he looked at her and said, "Give me some money."

She opened her purse and gave him $20 and said, "Jim you don't need anything to drink."

"I don't need anything?" he said with sarcasm in his voice.

And then he just looked at her and got up to go buy his liquor. He returned a few minutes later with the bag and it contained a 5th of Gin, a 6 pack of beer and cigarettes. He got in the car and his wife pulled off to go down the road. It seemed to go on forever, her mind fixed on this man to her right, but her eyes never left the road. She felt an impending doom that chilled her to the bone.

The Smiths arrived home only to find that she left the door open. Jim had a fit and smacked his wife in the face.

"The next time you make sure you lock the door, someone could have came in here and wiped us out," Jim said as he sat down and took a sip of his bottle of Gin.

Jane is frightened by her husband's act of aggression and anger that is kindled against her. In addition, the phone rang as soon as they got in the door. Normally he would tell her not to answer it and that he would get it, but this night was different. She hesitated before picking up the phone because she was expecting to hear him say that he would get it, and when he didn't say anything she knew something was in the air. She could feel it like a thick fog. However, Jim is sitting in his favorite chair in front of the television with his drink and his shotgun at his side. In the meantime, Jane is on the phone. It was Fran calling to see how her mother was doing after she had Jim arrested.

"Hey, Mom what's going on?" Fran asked.

"Not too much," she replied, "I'm scared."

"Why?" Fran asked.

"Because of your father, he's acting strange."

"What he's doing now?" Fran asked.

"He's watching TV and drinking and that's a bad combination. And do you know what he told me?"

"What?" Fran replied.

"He told me he can't go to prison at his age and that he would die first. And I believe him," she said.

As Jane is talking to Fran on the telephone, her husband is also on the telephone listening to everything being said, and he hangs up before they noticed he was listening.

"I'm coming to get you right now Mom," said Fran.

"Okay Dear," her mother replied.

"I will be right there."

"Hurry up," she replied and then hangs up. Jim is sitting in his chair drunk with a bottle in one hand and his gun in the other.

He then calls to his wife in a non-agitated voice, "Jane can I speak to you for a moment?"

The way he called her scared her more than anything. It was like he became someone else. So, she acted like she didn't hear him, so he called again now agitated and scared her out of her trance.

"Jane bring your Ass in here right now and don't make me come and get you!"

"I'm coming, what is it?" Jane asked him.

"I want to talk to you," he said to her as she walks into the room. He then tells her to sit down.

She does, but notices the shotgun on his lap and asked, "What are you doing with that gun?"

He quickly replied, "That's the reason I want to talk to you. I told you I can't go to prison and I'm not; I will die tonight and I can't live without you. If I go to prison they will kill me anyway."

"I don't want to die with you," Jane said as she started crying.

She immediately begs for her life with tears in her eyes and then she said, "I have to go to the bathroom."

"Don't you move!" he yelled.

"But I have to go!" she yelled back to him.

Then with an evil grin on his face, he told her, "Go in your Fucking pants."

Jane was frozen with fear. Then she broke her fear and moved a little.

And Jim quickly yelled, "I told you don't Fucking move! If I have to kill you where you sit, I will!"

"Please let me go," she said as she cries and begs a man who has lost everything, and she knows that her life means nothing to him because he doesn't care about his own.

"I wish Fran would get here soon. But, when she comes he might kill me and her," she thought to herself as she watched him closely waiting to make her move towards the door. He then drops his head. So, Jane took off towards the door. And with his finger on the trigger, he shot her twice in the back. She died in a pool of blood.

Jim went to check on her then went back to his seat, took a drink, smoked a cigarette and watched a little TV waiting for Fran to come in. A few moments later he heard someone yelling. It was Fran calling for her mother. When she walked in the door her father was holding the gun under his chin. Then she sees her mother on the floor dead from shots to the back. Fran started yelling and screaming for him to also kill her.

But he just looked at her and said, "I'm not going to kill you. I want you alive so you can suffer. I should kill you, but that's too easy. I want you to remember this day for the rest of your life."

Then he pointed the gun at his chin and pulls the trigger, blowing his head off. Parts of his brain was sticking to the wall and ceiling. He cheated her out of vengeance. And he was right, Fran would never forget this day. It was a crime scene right out of the movies and Fran had a front row seat. Or it was a nightmare she could not awake from? The thought of her mother's tragic death would ride shotgun with her all the days of her life.

The police arrived 10 minutes after Jim Smith took his life. They had to scrape his brain and bone fragments up with a metal scraper. It was a dirty job and it took 3-hours to clean up the crime scene.

The next day they reported the story in the newspapers about a murder-suicide. They wanted to put Fran's picture in the papers, but she did not want them to because of her husband's business dealings, and his inside connections. Also, she did not want a scandal to erupt about her sexual abuse because she wanted to keep that private. It also gave her comfort that her mother did not have to suffer anymore at the hands of her father.

LESSON 7

One Monkey Don't Stop NO Show

It was a sad day when Fran buried both of her parents; Jane and Jim Smith. Then she started blaming herself for her mother's death because if she did not report the crime to the police her mother would still be alive. Her grandson would never meet his grandmother, but he will know how wonderful she was through his mother and her beautiful memories. And through the many pictures she has and the ones that she keeps tenderly in her heart. But the ones of her father she tried to exclude them like a rainy day. But the thought of him always slips in with the sweet ones of her mother Jane. Fran buried her mother away from her husband. *"He did not deserve to be with her," she thought to herself as her mother's casket was being lowered into the ground.* At that time, she began to weep. Bill held his wife and told her everything will be alright. Then she melted and his confidence that she would make it through this most difficult time in her life. She yearned for a better life and happiness, although her mother won't be there to share it with her. She won't be there with her as she grows to become a woman in the full glory of herself; a woman of elegance and beauty.

The many family and friends that were present began to leave the cemetery, but Fran and Bill stayed behind.

"Let me say my goodbyes alone," she said to him.

"I will be in the car," he replied. She shook her head as he walked away.

"Mom I'm going to miss you very much," she said as she began to cry once more, "until we meet again, a day will not pass without me thinking of you. I love you, Rest in Peace." Then she dropped a rose into the ground and walked away.

It was September 15, 1972, Bill Freeman was just arriving at a Replacement Station of the 101st Airborne. He was drafted for a six-month tour of Vietnam in which he did not want to go. He thought his money will keep him out of this war, but he was wrong. He could have gotten on a plane and went to another country, but he risks going to prison and he did not want to do that. But the hell he was about to go through made prison seem like a walk in the park, besides he heard the food was Shit on a plate. He would have to take his chances in the jungles of Vietnam.

Colonel Joe Reagan was giving a pep talk, "Good evening gentlemen, welcome to Hell on Earth, you are about to go where you've never gone before. You are about to see what you've never seen before. And you are about to experience something that you've never experienced. This is a war men where the shadow death will follow you everywhere. Some of you will not make it back alive. But I promise you this, I will bring you home dead or alive." *Bill said to himself, "That makes me feel good to know that Bullshit."*

The Military Police also welcomed the plane load of arrivals to the country and then said, "Go directly to the buses, in case of a rocket attack on the base or ambush during transport."

Immediately Bill's legs began to shake, thinking that he would never make it home to his crazy wife and his brat son. Nevertheless, he missed them even though they drove him up the wall, but he loved them just the same. He thought of Fran and how she would call him all kinds of bad names. And how his son would tell him to Fuck Off.

The first-time Bill saw a dead body he threw up. A guy had gotten his head blown off with an M60 Machine Gun and it was not a pretty sight. He was killed as he walked in the line of friendly fire. Some of the men thought he was high on something. Bill also thought about who would run his business if he dies in this war. Fran would blow all his money up on shoes. His wife was still young and had a lot to learn about life. She does not even cook, how would she run a multimillion dollar business? The lawyers will take the company for millions in fees. The money would change Fran for bad or good; the bottom line is, she would change.

The day came when Bill's Platoon went on a mission. It was to remove the enemy from a village where the Vietcong had set up and to confiscate weapons. A force of 80 men snuck through the jungle trying to distract the enemy that were waiting to kill any American they saw. And the GI's managed to get by.

LT Bart Simpson said, "This is too easy, this must be a setup." But they kept moving forward.

They had two Huey Helicopters on standby, just in case things got out of control. The men reached the village and they were met by enemy fire in which seven men were killed. It was an ambush, the Vietcong let the Americans past so they reach the village. And the Vietcong behind them could come forward and they would be trapped in the middle. It was hell, Bill was on his back trying not to get hit by bullets coming from all directions. Sadly, the guy on Bill's left caught one right between the eyes and he slumped onto Bill with his eyes wide open. He is terrified from the blood and gore all around him.

He thought to himself, "I will never be the same after this Shit." And he was not far from the truth.

LT Bart Simms yells to the communication's man, "Call for air support and blow the whole Fucking village up. I can't afford to lose any more men!"

Ten minutes later jet fighters dropped their load and blew the village sky high. There was nothing left but body parts and burning bamboo. The death toll was high for the Vietcong. At least 300 men were killed that day along with 30 Americans. However, Bill Freeman survived, he would live to fight another day. He also was elected to collect the dead, it was a dirty job, but someone had to do it.

So, he picked up one body and the guy had no legs or arms. Bill had to look for his body parts a few feet away. The poor guy stepped on a landmine and went to pieces. Bill could not find one of his legs, but he was determined to find it. LT Simms told him to consider that leg missing in action or just put any leg in the bag, who would know.

"I would," Bill said.

"If you want to search for one leg all Fucking day then you go right ahead. And if you get your Fucking Head Blown Off, don't say I didn't warn you!" LT Simms yelled.

"I understand Lieutenant, what's next Sir," he quickly said.

"You help these other guys load these body bags on the helicopter and let's get the Fuck out of here," the lieutenant responded.

"Yes Sir," he replied.

It was December 24th, Christmas Eve and this would be the first Christmas Bill would be away from his family. Also, he didn't have worry about putting any coal in Tony's stocking, anyway he'd rather hit him with it.

Later that day, Bill was sitting and waiting on the mail call to see if his wife wrote him a letter.

Then the sergeant called, "Freeman you have a letter."

He received the letter and sat down to read it.

> Hello Sweetheart,
>
> I hope by the time you receive this letter you're not dead, but if you're reading this letter you're alive and well. I miss you and when are you coming home? I miss beating you up or you letting me beat you up. Tony is no fun. I'm kidding.
>
> I'm running low on cash, so can you call the bank to authorize a withdrawal. And if you don't do it, when you come home I'm going to shoot you with your own gun.
>
> I hope you're not messing around over there and bring me back the clap. So, keep it in your pants or get with Mary Palmer and her five sisters. You know them very well. Love you see you soon.
>
> Oh Merry Christmas
>
> Love Fran
>
> XOXOXOXOXOXO

Bill wrote the bank and told them to give Fran the money she wanted. I've been in Vietnam for 3 months and I'm still alive, but that could change in a New York minute. He is talking to Mike Jones a Black guy from Philadelphia Pennsylvania who loves smoking marijuana.

Mike said, "If I die, I want to be so high because I don't want to see it, and I don't want to feel it." Then he went to pass Bill the Joint.

"I don't do drugs," Bill replied.

"You should, so when that little girl or boy with the picnic basket offers you a Coke or Pepsi and blows your Fucking Balls off you will wish you were high then," said Mike.

Bill replied, "Trust me if it happens I want to be clear-headed dealing with this killing Shit."

"Well, when that little girl or boy comes near me, I won't hesitate to blow their Fucking brains out or anybody who looks like them; I'm not taking any chances because I might die tomorrow so I'm getting Fucked up today," Mike said.

Bill slipped and said, "Your one Crazy Nigger."

"Who you calling a Nigger, Honky?"

"I'm sorry," Bill said feeling very apologetic.

But Mike is unforgiving and replied, "I'm going to put my foot so far up your Ass you're going to taste the Dog Shit that I stepped in last week. Bill did not know where that came from because he had never called a Black person a Nigger before, but for his slip up Mike caught him with an overhand right that landed on Bill's jaw, knocking him to the ground. The other GI's gathered around to watch the fight and the sergeant broke it up and told the two of them to settle down.

Then he asked, "What's this about?"

He called me a Nigger.

"Is that true?" he asked Bill.

"Yes," he replied.

"We don't call each other names like that because the same guy you call a Nigger might be the guy who saves your Ass out there, so get with the program fellas."

Bill would never use the 'N' word again. As a matter of fact, they became good friends until on a Recon Mission to obtain information by visual observation about the enemy.

On the mission, Mike was the point man, he took two steps into an uncharted jungle and all the sudden he was impaled by a booby trap with sharp bamboo that struck him in the head and in the back. Mike died instantly, it happened so fast. But Mike got his wish because he didn't see it and he definitely didn't feel it.

The two of them had become good friends and had plans of going into business together. But after the loss of his buddy, Bill did not get too close to anyone because they would probably be dead the next hour.

The war in Vietnam was a nasty one. Bill's tour was up a year later and he would have nightmares for the rest of his life.

Bill said goodbye to the guys and as he was about to board the helicopter Lt Bart Simms asked him, "Do you want to re-enlist for another year?"

"Fuck you and this war. I'm surprised you're not dead already because the life span for a lieutenant is 15 minutes in Vietnam. I'm going home, the only part of me you going to see is my White Ass getting on this chopper." And he did just that.

"I'm going back to peace and serenity. I want to die old, toothless and not buy some gook blowing my Fucking brains out," he thought to himself as he fell asleep for a long ride home.
He had one stop left before the ride back to the States without worring about being blown up. He has peace at last, now that he was on his way back to his family.

LESSON 8

Keep your Friends Close,
But Keep your Enemies Closer

It was almost year later since Bill left Vietnam, he thought he was alright from seeing all the death and bloodshed, but he started having nightmares. He was shell shocked and he knew something was wrong. He kept having the same dream every night in which he would see someone carrying his head. And he is telling the person in the dream to find his body before the maggots eat it down to the bone.

He would wake up screaming and yelling, "Don't eat my body!" soaking wet with sweat.

Fran tried to console him; sometimes she could and other times she couldn't. It became very stressful for her after Bill came home because he was not the same person he was before he left. The war changed him. A minute of hell can change you forever. The women and children he had seen murdered will always remain in the shadow of his memory for all time. Bill became very moody all the time and his wife wanted to kill him. He wouldn't give her a break and would tell her to get off his back about money. Fran would tell him that she needed something and he would tell her to get a job.

"I'm no Fucking bank!" he yelled.

"But you told me I would never have to work."

"I lied," Bill said.

"I won't have you treating me like this Bill."

"Save that for someone who gives a Rats Ass because I don't. I'm not the same person you married Fran," he said, "you deal with me like I am or

I will give you a First-Class Ticket back to your trailer park! You hear me!"
She was shocked by his words, they cut deep. So much so she couldn't even respond, she was speechless, but she found the words, "I want to help you through this, please let me help you."

He replied, "All you want to do is help yourself."

"That's not true Bill."

"You don't love me."

"I do," she said looking unaffected by his words.

"That would be news to me, tell me this when did you start?"

"What? After your son was born."

"I never had a chance to love anybody because my father hated me."

"I thought everybody else felt the same," she said, "I always had a shield around me for years. I would not let anybody love me because I hated myself for what my father did to me. But I'm learning to love you more every day."

Bill looked at her and said, "Is that so. I loved you before I met you; do you understand?"

"I want to work this out," she said.

He replied, "Work what out?"

"I know you heard that before so how does the shoe fit on the other foot?"

"Oh, you Bastard!"

"Love me or leave me," he said, "It's your choice so what it's going to be? Me or the trailer Park?"

"I think I will stick this out with you," she said.

"I thought you would see it my way. I want to know what's my son been up to these days."

"He has been pretty good since he started going out with that girl Jennifer Parker, he is with her most of the time like they're madly in love."

"Maybe he is," Bill said.

"I had to take him to court the other day."

"For what?" her husband asked.

"Tony took the car and hit somebody and kept going; so, the person he hit wrote down the license plate and gave the information to the police; one day they kept asking for you telling me they had a warrant for your arrest. I told them this must be a mistake because you were overseas fighting a war the USA was not going to win. I asked Tony did he know anything about the fender bender he then admitted that he did it. The police arrested him for driving without a license, joyriding and leaving the scene of an accident."

At that moment, Tony walked in, "Hey Dad."

"Don't hey dad me you Little Shit. I was going to treat you to something nice like buy you a new car to take your girlfriend out sometimes; you are 16, right?"

"Almost."

"It does not matter anyway you messed that up. The only thing I'm going to give you is my foot in your Ass the next time you mess up," Bill said. Tony could not believe his ears because his dad used to run over is not taking any Shit now.

"And if you don't like what I'm saying you could find some other place to live you got that Boy?"

"Yes Sir," Tony replied.

"I like the sound of that yes sir, as a matter of fact, I want both of you to address me as Sir you Maggots…got that?" *Fran looked at Bill with sympathy in her eyes and thought to herself, "He has lost his mind."*

The war had really messed Bills mind up and he was getting worse by the day. He would get in the shower with his boots on talking to himself saying that *Charlie could not get him in the shower.* But then he would say come get me, I have water to protect me, I got a bar of soap too, you dirty Sons of a Bitches. After he got tired of yelling, he would get out of the shower, get dressed, and go to work. Then he would come downstairs and ask Fran what's cooking in the Chow Hall, she would answer French Toast, bacon, and eggs Sir. I like that soldier you keep up the good work. I might promote you to shine my boots. Bill had turned his house and to a boot camp. Fran wanted to put him out of his emotional distress with a blunt object. The young woman needed him because he had money; she knew if he went completely crazy she would take over all his business affairs and his money so, she would play along with his game. Tony, on the other hand, did not like his father much because he would always ask him if he was a trader and if he was he helping Charlie who were Vietnamese soldiers. Also, because he would pat him down for weapons.

"You're Fucking Nuts Dad!"

"I told you to address me as Sir! Now repeat after me Maggot! You're Fucking Nuts Sir!" Tony repeated what is father said trying not to laugh, but Bill was really going crazy.

Tony and Fran sometimes put up with his Shit, but other times he wanted to kick his father right in the Balls. Bill called a meeting at his office, and all his employees were there.

"I'm calling this meeting to let all of you know that I will be stepping down as CEO of my company. I know all of you have heard that I'm not well. I can't do my job as well as I would like to so Dan Stevens will be taking over in my place. I have all the confidence in the world that he can do a good job. I will be checking in from time to time to see what's going on, I want to warn all of you if you fail to do your job I will not hesitate to replace you. If you think that you are not going to perform, I advise you to leave now and save me the trouble of firing you. I guess that's about it, so do your best and the job you save may be your own."

Bill started seeing a doctor for his nightmares, he was diagnosed with Post-Traumatic Stress Disorder also called it PTSD for short, which is caused by exposure to a traumatic event involving intense fear horror or helplessness usually involving death or serious injury to oneself or someone else. Symptoms come in groups, distressing nightmares or flashbacks, avoiding any thoughts of the event and the ability to recall the trauma, avoiding activities that used to bring pleasure, feeling detached or estranged from others, and ability to love. Difficulty sleeping increased irritability or outbursts of anger. Bill would have to work this out himself.

LESSON 9

You Must Love Yourself First,
Before You Love Another

It's winter and many years have passed since Fran's parents passed away. She thought of her mother every day after she died and still blames herself for her death. She often finds herself crying because of her and thinks how sweet and kind she was and it saddens her deeply. She hopes her father is burning in Hell for taking her mother from her, she knows she is in Heaven looking down on her.

Tony is 25-years-old now and he is going to the best college in the country, he also drives a Benz his father bought for him when he graduated from high school. He also is still in love with his childhood sweetheart Jennifer. They have been together since middle school, but with Tony cheating on her with other girls; their relationship will be tested. The two are always fighting because Tony has rich parents and he thinks he can do anything he wants and most of the time he does, he is a Spoiled Brat. The first time they had sex Tony told her she smelled like a toxic dump and then she slapped him in his face. He slapped her back and they started fighting naked until she ended the fight with a kick to his Balls. He fell to his knees in pain.

"I'm sorry, I was only playing," she replied.

"I was not playing! The next time you want to play call your Mother because I'm not in the mood for your childish games!" Tony yelled.

Tony and Jennifer will always make up before they had sex. It was an every week thing. Sometimes she would start an argument with Tony so he would slap her; she liked it in a Kinky kind of way. The kinkiness started showing when Tony noticed that he would hit Jennifer at least 3 to 4 times a week and in every case, she would start the fight.

He said, "You must like getting your Ass whipped."

"Maybe I do," the smiling woman said.

"I'm not going to feed into your Shit anymore, you're having too much fun and I'm not."

She told him that she was in the mood one night and they both had a little too much to drink. They were celebrating Jennifer finishing Law school. Then she grabbed his hand and pulled him into the room at her apartment, he laid her down on the bed as he fell in the sweetness of her breasts and hourglass figure made him weak for her sex.

She told him to tie a rope around her neck and pull it tighter every time he thrust inside her. She moaned with passionate anguish as he choked her with Perverted Ecstasy.

"GIVE IT TO ME!" she screams, "pull it tighter you Wimp!"

"Who you calling a Wimp?" he asked as he pumps her sex. She can't talk because of the tightness of the rope, but she manages to get the word 'TIGHTER' out as he reaches his Climax. Jennifer falls into the bed on her stomach.

Tony asked, "How was that?" She didn't repond.

"You alright?"

He turns her over and realizes she's not breathing, so he starts to panic and gives her CPR. After a few minutes of pumping her chest and some mouth to mouth, she started breathing on her own and she opened her eyes.

He asked again, "Are you alright?"

"Yes. Let's do that again."

"You're crazy, I'm not doing that again, so don't ask me; you almost died and I was on my way to prison for life," he said.

"I have never had an orgasm in my life like that, you are my sexual hero, you have saved me from a dual sex life, I'm hooked! I will never have sex without a rope again."

"You're Warped, "Tony said.

"You can't say that you did not enjoy it too."

"I must admit it was a little bit frightening and dangerous to get off like that. Let's do it again Jennifer."

"Come on!" she said.

"You're sick, you need help."

"I'm kidding never again in a million years; you can always choke yourself."

"It's not the same."

"Oh well, I'm done with that kind of sex."

Tony started working with his father's business delivering documents and mail to businesses doing work for the firm. He travels all over the city. What he likes about his job, he has his own hours as long as he gets done by 5pm so, he has the whole day to do what he wants.

The time came when he got lost in a bad section of town. He saw a fellow standing on the corner, he stopped him and asked for directions.

"How can I get to 24 Thatcher Street?"

The man responded, "You're on the wrong side of town." The man's name was Lexington Flowers. He then asked for a ride.

"Can I show you how to get there for a small fee?"

"How much are you going to charge me for giving me a ride to where you live?"

"I don't live over there; I work over there."

"How about 20 bucks."

"That's cool," Lexington said.

"Alright get in." He gets in the car and slams the door.

"Come on man watch the door!"

"Oh, I'm sorry, this is a nice car."

"And your name?"

"Tony."

"Glad to meet you, I'm Lexington." The two men shook hands.

"So, what are you doing around here?"

"I'm lost remember."

"Oh, that's right, so what kind of work do you do?"

"I'm a messenger working part time."

"That's all?"

"So, what kind of work do you do?" Tony asked.

"I'm a doorman at a gentleman's club."

"What's the name of the club?"

"Bottoms Up, I got VIP tickets for sale; you want to buy one?"

"You should give me one free, for the ride."

"I'm already giving you $20 for helping me." Lexington took Tony to drop off is mail on 24th Street and then dropped him off at the club.

"Thank you for the ride."

"I will try to come by one day."

"Alright, where's my free tickets?"

"Oh I forgot. Here you go and be safe out there." Then the two men parted.

Tony dropped the rest of his mail off and went home. When he got home his mother was lying on the couch watching TV.

"Hey Mom, what's going on?"

"Your father is getting on my last nerve acting crazy again."

"What is he doing this time?"

"He locked himself in his room again telling me to call the President of the United States and call off the war or he's going to kill his hostage."

"He's Fucking Crazy! Mom we have to get help for him soon."

"I will as soon as I get the Power of Attorney."

"Mom you don't know how to manage money; his lawyers are fighting you now for control."

"But I would have it one day and you and I will be alright."

"They will never give you complete control of his money. Mom you should let me get some of it and I will take care of you."

She looked at him and said, "You're out of your Fucking mind you have a hard time wiping your own Ass so how are you going to run something?"

"I put up with his Shit all these years and I deserve my share of the money and you will get your share too."

"You just keep your nose out of business that don't concern you."

"This is my business."

"I will own everything one day you wait and see. I promise I won't put you in a nursing home, I will let you live behind my estate."

"I think you should get out of my face before I find something sharp and bury you out back."

One-day Bill ignited Fran's anger to a point she wanted to kill him. So, she offered to take him out for the day. She drove him to the shore. Fran and Bill were standing at the end of the pier and she wanted to push him in and get it all his money, but someone would question what was she doing at the shore that day. Besides someone would probably see her push him and she will lose everything.

"I wanna know, why have you brought me here?" Bill asked.

"It was a nice day."

"It was a nice day yesterday too, so whatever you're thinking don't try it."

"Try what?" she responded.

"I smell Treachery and Deceit all over you," he said as he looked in her eyes.

"I would never hurt you."

"That's just what you want to do so, I'm going home; you won't push me in the water today, Sweetie," he said and then he walked to the car.

"Come on Honey," he said as he got in the car. Fran followed him and got into the driver's seat looking like she saw a ghost.

"Fran let's stop and grab a bite to eat." She did not say a word letting him know she did have something planned.

LESSON 10

Drink Water Out of Your Own Lakes and Rivers
And Out of Your Own Well

It was September 3, 1984; Tony finished 3 years of college in Business Administration and was starting as a department manager at his father's company. His father would come and go as far as his mental condition was concerned. He would be alright one week and then the next week he would be completely out of his mind, but his mind never strayed too far from his money, his business or how it's being handled. Fran was telling her friend Betty who she met at a Black and White Ball in honor of her husband's work for the environment. He helped companies get Federal money for toxic dump cleanups. The fact is, that Betty and Fran became friends almost overnight, she is the wife of the Dark Water's CEO, Dan Stevens; the one Bill appointed to take his place. Betty told Fran that her relationship with her husband is on the rocks and he makes her sick; they never have sex.

"Well how do you release yourself," Fran asked.

"I have my Electronic Friend, that's the love of my life. It's better than Dan's crooked Dick. I don't ask him for sex. But every 6 months we may have it, other than that, I have my little Buddy. I think he's getting it from a prostitute. I should say I know he is. I caught him one time in a sleazy motel with two whores. I walked in on him with a diaper on and a baby bottle in his mouth. That's his fetish, he likes to dress up like a baby and Shit on himself and get a spanking for it. I've been a bad boy he tells the women and they take turns beating him with a belt. He pays $300 an hour for that service."

"I will beat his Ass for free," Fran said."

And the two women laughed at Dan thinking about how he looked dressed like a kid in a Shitty diaper. Betty asked Fran if she has ever been with an escort.

"What's that?" she asked.

"It's a male or female prostitute who will take you on a date. If you want to have sex with them you can, it's your choice."

"How much do they charge?"

"$200 an hour."

"That's a lot of money," Fran said,

"Have you ever had one?"

"Oh, yes and It's worth the money?"

"Do you know any good ones?" Fran asked.

"As a matter of fact, I do."

"What's his name?"

"Neno Perez, he's Spanish."

"Is he any good?" Fran asked.

"Yes, he is," Betty responded.

"I will call him later and set something up," said Fran. She got home about 6pm and Bill was in his study playing chess with himself.

He heard her come in, "Fran is that you?"

"Yes," she answered.

"Where have you been? I hope not somewhere spending my money."

"That's just what I was doing."

"How much did you spend?"

"About $500," she said.

"I'm going broke and you're wasting money, we need to control our spending because one of my investments fell through, my company lost 10 million dollars, the price of oil fell, and we are losing to overseas competition. We have to downsize and save some money."

"You have over 30 million the bank."

"So, what? At this rate, we won't have it if you keep throwing money away."

"I have something to say; I want a divorce because you don't love me anyway, all I want is 10 million dollars and let me go on my own way."

"Hell No! I won't let you go; I will save money keeping your Ass with me."

"I need a drink," Fran said.

She went to the bar and got a shot of Beefeater Gin. After the hour, she was feeling real good and thought of using the number that Betty gave her; she had it in her bag.

Then she called it and Neno answered, "Hello this is Neno speaking."

"This is Miss F, I would like to use your services if I may."

"When and where would you like to meet?"

"We can meet at the Ram Motel about 1 in the morning if you're not too busy."

"I'm free."

"Do you know where the motel is?"

"Yes," he said.

"I will see you then," and she hangs up.

It's 1am Fran is sitting in her car waiting and a handsome Spanish guy comes to the car and he asked, "Are you Miss F?"

"Yes, I am," she said.

"How are you doing? You must be my date, you're a very pretty lady."

"I want you to please me and you will."

"That's why I'm here," he said.

"I want to get something straight, I don't want to know you; all I want is to have sex and get home to my husband. You got that Hector?"

"My name is Neno."

"Whatever."

The two entered the room and had sex for a few hours and then Fran went home. She paid $400 for his services. Bill would kill her for spending that money, he could care less about her having sex with another man. It was 4am when Fran got in, Bill was asleep. Fran crept up to the bedroom, took off her clothes, got into bed and fell asleep. She dreamt of that strange man touching her places Bill would never go in her dreams or in real life.

The next day, Fran called Betty and told her what happened the night before.

Her friend asked, "How was it?"

"It was great and Neno is so good looking."

"So how was the sex?"

"It was real good."

"I know you will be calling him again."

"I might be, who knows I have to watch out for Bill; he was up when I got in last night. I won't call him for a while."

"Yeah right," Betty said, "I can see your smile through the phone."

"I am married remember." The two women laughed about the whole thing.

"I can't treat my husband like that," Fran said.

"I have to go, I have some work to do," Betty told her.

"I'll talk to you later, bye."

The fight started when Bill went through Fran's purse looking for the keys to the car; he searched all through it and then stopped when he found a condom. *He said, "What the hell is this?" to himself and then he called Fran.*

She answered, "What is it?"

"I found something in your purse."

"What the hell are you doing in my bag anyway?"

"I was looking for the keys and found this!" He held up the condom out so that she could see it.

She was about to tell him off until she saw what was in his hand. "I can explain."

"Explain what? That you are Whore?"

"Who are you calling a Whore?"

"You," he replied, "you're the one with the condom in your purse, you add it up."

"I could not get sex from you so I went someplace else."

"So, you know how I felt when you were spoon feeding me sex. I want you out of this house," Bill said.

"This is my house too; I'm not going anywhere. You get all bent out of shape because I gave away a little Pussy. I know you were Fucking the housekeeper for years; you thought I didn't know."

"That's not true!" he yelled.

"So, if it's not true, tell me why you fired her and hired another housekeeper? I'm going to tell you why because you got her pregnant and then you told her you didn't need her anymore and gave her $50,000 to go away someplace to keep quiet."

"How did you know that?"

"I found a withdrawal slip about the same time she left. I can divorce your Ass and take half of what you own so, this house is mine. So, ask me can you stay."

He looked at her and said, "Can I stay?"

Fran said, "I will think about it. I got you by your Balls and you will pay."

Bill really stuck his foot in his mouth he should have kept it shut knowing he has skeletons in his closet. She had dirt on him and all the soap in the world could not wash off.

The housekeeper has been gone for 3 years and the baby was that old. Fran knows that Bill has a baby somewhere in the world. If she had the baby or she got an abortion, she would find out.

LESSON 11

If a Wise Man Sees Danger He Hides Himself from It,
But the Fool Goes to Suffer for It

The gentlemen's club opens at 8pm; Tony was there at 7pm with his VIP pass that Lexington gave him last week.

Lexington met him at the door, "I see you made it."

"I could not miss this for the world," he said.

"Who are your feature dancers tonight," he asked.

"Dark Chocolate, Danger, Satin, and Sweetness," he replied.

"I will take all of them," he said jokingly with a big smile.

"I know you brought a lot of cash so, you'll get your chance later."

"I hope so," he answered.

Tony went in and sat down in the VIP section. The music they played was soft and smooth. The man announced the first the dancer who was Satin who came on the stage in a glittery thong, red stilettos with her beautiful mocha chocolate color legs. Her luxurious breasts peeked out behind the same material she wore and then she began to dance around the pole as she opened and closed her legs to reveal her perfectly trimmed Twat. Tony felt an erection coming on as he sipped his glass of Cognac. Two women came over to his table; both were a soft sensual brown with fine bodies. The first woman asked him did he want any company as she bent over shaking her Ass in his face.

"The both of you are beautiful, but I'm straight."

"Can I give you a lap dance."

"I'm cool, maybe later."

The other women pulled one of her breasts out and licked her nipple and asked, "You want to taste the other one?"

"No thank you," he quickly replied, as he was watching Satin on stage still performing.

They noticed that his eyes were on the woman on the stage so, they walked away to the next table. He then got up and walked toward the stage and put a $20 bill in her G-string as she opened her legs to let him see it all.

She said, "You like what you see?"

"Yes, I do," he answered.

"You can see a whole lot more if your money's right."

"How much is it going to cost?"

"Let me finish up here and then we will talk." Tony went back to his table and sat down, he then waved for the waitress.

She came over and asked, "Can I help you?"

"What is your name?" he asked.

"Treasure," she replied.

"And you are that. I would like a 5th of Hennessy and two glasses please."

"Can I party with you tonight?" she asked.

This woman was gorgeous; she was Spanish and Black mixed, thick legs with nice breasts and luscious lips. *"She looked better than Satin," he thought to himself.*

"I made plans already," he answered.

At that moment, Satin walked up and set right on Tony's lap and looked at Treasure right in her eyes and said, "Don't you have work to do?" The woman rolled her eyes and walked away.

"That's not nice," he said.

"It don't pay to be nice, but it's nice to pay," she said as she grabbed Tony's hand and lead him down a hallway to the room in the back of the club where you can hear women moaning from men spending their money to get their Rocks Off.

The two entered the room; the only thing in there was a small bed and a chair. He sat on the bed.

She said, "Let's talk money, what do you want?"

"Everything I can get," he answered.

"I like you a little bit so I'm going to say $300. You alright with that?"

He shook his head without saying the word as he reached to touch her smooth legs.

She smacked his hands and said, "No pay no play." Then he reached for his wallet and took out three 100 bills and gave it to her.

"Fair exchange is no robbery now you can touch me. You got one hour to do whatever, I'm not into that kinky Shit. I got somebody outside the door just in case you get Crazy."

"I'm not that kind of person."

"Good, let me dance for you because the clock is running."

She started dancing exotic, swaying her hips as she stripped nice and slow. She bent over shaking her round Ass in Tony's face, then she began to rub her breast, he was about to explode in his pants, but contained himself. Satin dropped her G-string to the floor as she was touching herself all over. Then she sat on Tony's lap and began to grind on his Erect Man. He started to shake as he grabbed the sides of the bed. Satin began to talk dirty to him saying, "Give it to me Baby," as Tony busted in his pants.

"Damn you Came that fast? You won't last a minute if I put this Twat on you."

"Yeah right," he said as he grabbed one of her breast.

"So, what do you want me to do now?"

"Nothing get dressed. I forgot I have to pick someone up."

"Who? Your wife?"

"Something like that."

Tony went to the restroom to wash his hands and clean himself up. Satin gave him her number and said, "Call me," then she said, "when you get tired of holding on to your money give me a call. I will take all you got."

"I know you will," he said looking at her beautiful everything.

Tony left the club in love with a stripper. He started thinking about his wonderful Jennifer. He gets home about 2am tired and ready to lay down but she was up waiting for him.

"What happened to you tonight?"

"I had to work late."

"Why didn't you call me and tell me you were not coming."

"I forgot."

"That's no excuse."

"Well, that's all I have right now, I will talk to you in the morning; goodnight." And turns over and goes to sleep.

The next day he called Satin; her real name was Renay Benson and she stayed with her mother on the West Side of the city. The young girl grew up fast. Her mother was addicted to cocaine. She had to fend for herself most of the time because her mother would blow her whole check on drugs. So, as she got older, the streets became her provider. Renay would sell drugs, sell her body, rob, and steal to get what she needed. When she was selling drugs, her mother stole her stash and she beat her mother up. She would have called the cops, but she was so high she did not care. The young woman became a product of her environment and she knew the streets well.

Tony dialed the phone and an older woman picked up, "Is this Satin?" he asked.

"Hold on," the women said, "telephone Renay."

"Who is it?"

"Who's calling?" the older women asked.

"Tony," he answered.

"Some guy named Tony; you want me to tell him you're not here?"

"No, I want that call…hello, what's up," she said, "you want to see me tonight?"

"No, I want to see you now if I can."

"I'm getting my hair done right now, but I should be done in about 2 hours; you can come scoop me up then."

"Alright," he said.

"Talk to you then, bye." And she hung up.

"I'm in love with a stripper," he thought to himself. She stole his heart in one night and that could mean trouble.

Two hours passed and Renay told Tony how to get to her house; he arrived about 5pm on Monday; she was all he thought about. When he got up that morning he did not say anything to Jennifer and she did not say anything to him because he had another woman on his mind.

When he pulled up she was standing outside looking fine as ever with her big brown eyes. She wore a sleeveless blouse that was Champagne colored and Capri Jeans with 4" high Platform shoes. Tony jumped out to go and open the door for her.

"Oh, a gentleman with money, I like that," she said as he held her hand as she sat down in the car. He closed the door and got in himself.

"This must be my lucky day."

"Why do you say that?" she asked.

"Because to be in this car with a woman as fine as you, I know I'm getting some of that Candy."

"If I look like candy, you want a bite?"

"I sure do."

"When you eat it, leave some for the next guy."

"I don't know, I'll try."

"But for real, though if your money is right we got all night."

"Sounds good to me. How much are you going to charge me for that Sweet Chocolate?"

"200.00," the smiling women said, "and I also take tips."

"I'm sure you do; I'll just give you $300.00. How about that?"

"Sounds like a party to me, I'm worth every dollar. You'll find out after you taste this, you won't want another woman."

"Is the sex like that?" Tony said as he pulled off down the street. Tony asked Renay were did she want to go to get something to eat.

She answered, "I don't care…oh on second thought, I want some fried chicken." So, they went to KFC and talked.

While they were eating, a guy came to their table and said, "Satin, how come you don't return my phone calls?"

Satin looked at the man up and down and said, "I don't owe you no explanation and you're not my man so, get out of my face."

"And this dude is?" he asked.

"Whoever he is or he's not, it's none of your business." He then looked at Tony and walked away.

"What was that about?" Tony asked.

"That was nothing, just one of my fans getting out of control."

"I see you have a strange effect on men being Beautiful, Black, and Sexy. Is he obsessed with you?"

"I don't think so."

"A man that has an obsession with any living thing he will eventually kill it."

"Is that so?"

"Yes, I just hope he does not get that far," he said looking real concerned.

The two finished eating and he asked Renay did she know of any good motels? She answered, "I sure do, as a matter of fact, make a right, turn on Broom Street and go 3 blocks down; the motel is on the right side; you can't miss it. It's a big white building." So, they proceeded to go to the motel.

"I guess I should go pay for the room."

"Your guess is right," the woman said, "I'm here to make money not to spend it. I need all mine." He then pays for the room and they get one in the back so no one would notice Tony's car because he does have a girlfriend. The two get out of the car, he opens the door, "Ladies first." As she goes in he is looking at her Round Ass and bites his finger in his excitement and then slaps her Butt.

Then she said, "Don't touch until you pay up."

"I'm going to hit it so good you're going to want to give my money back."

"Hell Naw, it's not going down like that." They arrived at the motel ready to go. As soon as they got in the room Tony grabbed Satin and kissed her.

She pushed him back, "Slow up man you didn't pay me yet."

"I'm good from the last time, right?"

"No, that was then, this is now. Besides, I want to start this off right; I might make you my man."

"Is that, right? I have someone, but I have room for you in my life."

"I don't care who you have, just take care of this and you'll be fine."

Tony starts taking off his clothes, "I'm ready."

"I see," she said. Satin went in her pocketbook and pulled out a bottle of Hennessey.

"I brought a little something to drink to set the mood. Care for some?" she asked.

"Sure, why not, I need something to help me tear it up."

"Yeah right, I'ma have some fun with you White Boy, you're going to be my best customer."

"If I become your man I'm not paying for sex anymore."

"I'm not free, she said, "you got to pay to play. Baby you are going to pay for this Pussy." Then she puts her finger on his lips and said, "Shut up and enjoy the show."

She starts dancing real slow and sexy, swaying her hips while taking her clothes off. Tony's on the bed with a smile and a hard-on, "Show me what you're working with."

"You see it, Baby?" By this time, she's naked. Tony begins kissing her up and down her body as she moans.

Then she lays down on the bed and opens her legs and said, "You have to get it Wet, and you have to Lick it before you Stick it." He went right to work on her sex, Licking, and Sucking. He was going crazy.

Then she said, "Hold up, Stop!"

"What's wrong?"

"Don't BITE, Lick it NICE and SLOW and stop biting me."

"I'm sorry."

"As a matter of fact, let me do you."

She gets up and starts giving him a Blow Job. She was making Slurping sounds. Tony is making lite moans saying, "I LOVE YOU, I LOVE YOU." She did it for about 5 minutes and she stopped before he Came. Then she opened her legs to receive him. He started pumping real fast, kissing her in the mouth. She turned her face because she did not want to kiss. So, he started Sucking on her breast and he Came in 2 minutes.

She said, "Hell No! Did you Come?"

"Sure did."

"Damn! I didn't even get mine, you Minute Man, it's alright, I guess I will get my Nut when you give me my $400.00."

"I said $300.00."

"I didn't get to Come so, you got to pay me." He looked at her and said no problem and gave her the money.

"It was nice doing business with you. And I'm serious about making you my man if you're up for the job," she said looking into his eyes.

"And what does this job pay?"

"This Good Pussy and my time; and you are required to work overtime when you are up in this and not No 2 Minute Shit either," Satin kissed him on his lips and said, "let's get out of here."

Tony said, "Hold up for a second. Let me ask you something?"

"What?"

"Do you have a man?"

"Yes," she answered.

"Who is he?"

"You, I didn't have one until now."

"Alright," he said, "but I have someone."

"I don't care about that as long as you take care of me, you can have as many someones as you want."

"I can live with that," he said smiling.

Tony and Satin left the motel; he dropped her off home and then he went home himself where Jennifer is waiting once again.

LESSON 12

What You Sow, You Shall Also Reap

Bill made a phone call to his former housekeeper Nancy Lopez, to find out how his son was doing. He was having sex with her every day for a year when Fran was not in the house. She almost caught him having sex with her a few times. But every time Bill would play it off like nothing was happening, but Fran knew; she just did not say anything. *She thought to herself, that she had bigger fish to fry and Bill would be her biggest fish of all.* He told Nancy that he would send her money for his son. She told him thank you and she still loves him. And he answered, he loved her too and he heard a 'CLICK' before he hung up, but thought nothing of it. He then said goodbye to his mistress and they hung up. The fights between Fran and Bill really heated up after that phone call with Nancy. Fran heard the entire conversation between them. She got so fed up with Bill that she went and filed for divorce. She wanted half of Bill's money and the house they lived in. She recorded Bill's conversation with Nancy and she gave it to her lawyer to use in her case. The lawyer told her she could win her case hands down. Bill would have to settle out of court and the tape would put the icing on the cake.

Six months passed by and Nancy stopped in to see her former boss because she needed money again.

Fran came in the house while Nancy was there and asked her, "What are you doing here Whore and your Bastard son?"

"Who are you calling a Whore You Crazy Bitch."

"I guess you feel real special that you have a son by my husband, I'm going to take him for everything he has and you won't get a dime," Fran said, "I would be wrong if I Beat your Ass."

And then Nancy smacked Fran in the face and Fran smacked Nancy back and they started fighting, throwing things, scratching, biting and tearing the house up.

Bill tried to break them up, "What are you doing Fran?"

"I'm going to teach this Bitch a lesson."

They continued to fight until Nancy picked up a metal vase and hit Fran over the head knocking her out cold. Bill went into a fit telling Nancy she killed Fran.

"You Fucking killed her!" he yelled.

"She's not dead, she's just knocked out."

"How do you know she's not dead?"

"Because I hear her snoring that's why," she said. Bill knelt down and started smacking Fran lightly on the face until woke up.

She opened her eyes and asked, "What happened?"

"You were knocked out by Nancy."

"Where is she?"

"I sent her home." Fran felt a little dizzy and had a little lump on her head, but she was fine.

"I'm going to have her arrested."

Bill said, "Leave it alone."

"I will not," she replied, "what are you protecting your little Whore."

"I just want this to go away, I want some peace again. I knew you were faking when you were acting crazy."

"I had you going didn't I," Bill said.

"You were only fooling yourself because I knew you were full of Shit and so, did Tony."

"Speaking of Tony, where is he?"

"I have not seen him in a couple of days, he has been acting strange. I think he has another girlfriend; someone has been calling herself Satin that called here."

"Sounds like a stripper to me," Bill said.

"Don't skip the subject, I want your little girlfriend to go to jail. Then you can bail her out Mr. Money Bags," Fran said, "I have a date tonight, you have a problem that?"

"No I don't; you can get him to put ice on your head," Bill said, "you're a free woman."

"I have been free our whole marriage, the 10 million made it official."

"Don't spend it all in one place," said Bill.

"I won't. I want to know when are you leaving my house?" she asked.

"When I get good and ready," replied Bill.

"Oh, you put your Balls back on. I thought I took 'em with your money."

"You just keep pushing it, I'm going to start pushing back," Bill said.

"The only pushing you're going to do is yourself out of my house, you have a week," said Fran and then she left the house.

Fran had a date with her Escort Neno, who has been having sex with Fran for 6 months. They have been seeing each other three times a week. On one occasion, they had sex in the Heat of Passion and Fran let Neno have sex with her WITHOUT a CONDOM.

She said to him before he entered her, "You don't have anything, do you?"

"No Baby," he replied.

"I hope not because I would not want to catch anything."

Fran started picking up Neno at his house; he would get Fran to make stops in places where drugs were being sold. Fran did not know that Neno was shooting up drugs; he would always be high on something when he was having sex with her. He even introduced her to cocaine.

He said, "Try this."

"What is that White Powder?" she asked.

"It's Cocaine," he answered.

"I don't do drugs," she said, "no, I don't want that. As a matter of fact, I won't be calling you again; you're a Junky, I'm leaving. How come you did not tell me?"

"Tell you what? I'm an addict and I needed the money," Neno said.

"How do you use it?" Fran asked.

"I shoot up."

"You what!?"

"I shoot up," he repeated.

"You mean to tell me I 've been having sex with you for 6 months and you're a Fucking Junky?"

"I'm No Junky"

"Wait right here for a moment," she said. She went to her car to get something.

"I have something to give you, I had it for somebody else, but you can have it now." When Fran came back to the room she had a long White box wrapped with a ribbon and a bow and started to open it.

Neno asked, "Who are those flowers for?" But it wasn't flowers, she pulled out a bat and started beating him on the head.

He screamed, "No Please! I'm Sorry!" As she beat him everywhere she could with tears in her eyes.

He cried out, "Also I'm sorry I did not tell you I have…" Then he fell out; he did not get the chance to finish his sentence.

Fran beat him to death out of anger and was sorry afterward. It was blood everywhere. She had it all over her clothes. She left and went to her car like nothing ever happened, but cried on her way home. Her life would never be the same and she knew it. What was Neno trying to tell Fran before she beat the last word out of him? The pain of not knowing what his dying words meant. *Hearing the words in her head 'I have' drove her crazy trying to solve the puzzle that Neno gave her.* The time came when Fran told Betty what she had done.

"I have to talk to you."

"When do you need to see me?" Betty asked.

"How soon can you come and meet me," replied Fran.

"I'm not doing anything now; I can meet you right now? Give me 10 minutes."

"I'll meet at Joanna's Food Stop on 29th and Kirk St," said Fran.

"Alright, I'll see you Then…bye." Betty arrived at Joanne's at 4:00.

"I'm glad you could come so soon," said Fran.

"You're my best friend, I'm here for you; you need me, you call me," replied Betty.

"I have done something I'm sorry about."

"What is it?" Betty asked.

"I killed Neno."

"You did what!?"

"I killed Neno."

"When!?"

"Two weeks ago."

"I saw that on the news, they said a man was found dead in a motel room beat to death. A witness said a White female was last seen leaving the room, but no one could identify her."

"I found out he was using drugs and we had sex without a condom and then he told me he shot drugs and I flipped out. I went to my car and got my bat and beat him everywhere. I could not stop until his life was gone; I did not mean to kill him."

As she started to cry, Betty hugged her and said, "Don't cry we are going to work this out."

"What shall I do? Should I turn myself in?"

"I don't know," replied Betty.

"I think I will turn myself in," Fran said, "I will get the best lawyer money can buy."

"I do have money, I will get you one and I will pay for it," said Betty, "I'm your friend and you're mine, I am with you until the end."

"What do you mean by that?" asked Fran.

"I'm your friend for life. When you cry, I cry; when you smile, I smile; when you laugh, I laugh, and when you're sad, I'm sad. God will help us through it, we just have to pray to Him. Jesus said come to Me all who labor and heavy laden and I will give you rest. Jesus loves you."

"I have never been the one to go to church, but I know God loves me, I want to go to church with you one Sunday Betty."

"That will be great, let's get out of here." They hugged and went home.

LESSON 13

The Rich Rules Over the Poor

And the Borrower is the Slave to the Lender

Tony and Jennifer were sitting at the dinner table.

"You don't treat me like you use to; I want to know why we don't go out anymore?" asked Jen, "do you still love me?"

"I still love you," Tony said.

"I don't want to live like this anymore when I don't have to. I want a life, and this is no life. Give me one reason to stay. If you love me, I can't see it, Tony," said Jennifer.

"I'm sorry for the way I have been treating you, I haven't been myself lately."

"Why?" she replied, "because of another woman?"

"No that's not it," said Tony.

"You lie in my face, we don't have sex that often if we do I have to get things started. If you want to be with someone else go be with her and let me go," she said and started to cry.

Tony said, "Alright I've been cheating, but I'm going to stop."

"When? After I leave your Ass?"

"I'm going to tell her today that I can't see her anymore."

"Who is she?" Jen asked.

"Just somebody I met," he replied.

"Do you love her?"

"I don't know?" Tony answered.

"You need to choose today and right now."

"I don't know?" he said again.

"Why do you want me here? You have broken my heart. I can't stay here when you don't know if you love this woman. The more love you have her is the less you have for me," Jen stands up and walks to the door and said, "until you can love me, the person who was there for you from the start and not somebody who you just met, stay away from me. I will pick my things up later." And slams the door and leaves.

Tony feels bad that he hurt Jennifer; he is moved by her sadness and wants to make things right. But his love for Satin will be tested to its limits.

Tony rented an apartment for Renay, the rent was $600 a month. Not long after Renay moved from her mother's place, her mother got evicted because Renay paid most of the rent and now she had no help. So, Renay let her mother come to stay with her, she did not like it, but it was her mother and she could not see her on the street. But at times her privacy would be invaded. If someone came over Renay's she would tell her to take a walk until she got done doing whatever or she would tell her to go to her room. Tony had a key so, one day he went to the apartment. Renay was not there so he unlocked the door and when he went in, he saw Renay's mother smoking crack, but she could not see him.

He walked in, "What do we have here?"

"Oh, hey Tony."

"Having fun?"

"What do you think? Want some?"

"I never tried it before."

"Here," she replied as she handed him the pipe and lit it.

He inhaled the smoke and Tony got a feeling that he never had in his life. Tony felt like he was in Heaven, but he was about to catch hell. While

Tony was high, Renay's mother pulled out more crack and Tony wanted more.

"I don't have much left," she said.

"Do you need money to get some?" Tony asked.

"Yes, I do."

"How much?"

"A hundred."

Tony heard the door open and it was Renay returning home. She walked in and saw Tony. "I know you're not in here getting high," said Renay, "damn mom, you gave him that first hit. Tony, you're a grown man give me some of that."

Renay smoked too, but she never told Tony because she did not know how he would take it. If she knew that, she would have gotten him hooked a long time ago. Tony became addicted, he started to blow thousands of dollars a week.

Fran said, "Tony, what's wrong with you? You're losing a lot of weight. Are you smoking that Shit?"

"No Mom," he replied.

"You're doing something. I checked your bank account; you took out $5000. What did you do with all that money?"

"I'm using," he admitted.

"I knew it," said Fran.

Tony's father took all his credit cards and froze his accounts so he could not waste any more money. Renay still had her apartment and Tony wrecked his car and his mother would not give him any more money. Renay told Tony that she had to make some money. Renay lost a lot of weight, also she started selling her body again. The drugs really took Tony where we had never been before. He was lost and he did not have his families' money to help him out.

A whole year went by and Tony was still getting high and Tony and Renay had a son, his name was Mark. Tony loved his first son. Therefore, Tony never called Jennifer back, but he sees her and she tells him that she still loves him and she is waiting for him to get his life back on track. Tony moved in with Renay and her mother; three addicts in one house is a recipe for disaster. Renay would go out to make money so that they could get high, but they would take care of their son. Tony would take Mark over to Fran's house sometimes and she wanted to keep him. Renay said it was fine because she could not take care of him because of her addiction. Renay and Tony started to fight all the time and Tony would beat her up over drugs and money or he would get jealous if Renay brought someone to the apartment to have sex for drugs. Tony had money, but his family cut him off for a while to teach him a lesson. But it was a hard lesson and he began to see the light. He was coming around, but it would take a long time. Bill wanted to talk to his son and tell him to get help, but Tony did not want help; not at this time.

"How did you start using drugs?" his father asked.

"I met a girl, also the mother of your grandson."

"Mark…he is a fine boy, he has my eyes," said Bill, "I will set up a Trust Fund for him just like I did for you, but your money is no good to you right now. I will return everything to you once you get some help. Until then, I will not give you one dime."
"But how will I live?" Tony asked.

"I don't know, you work it out Son," he said as he put his hand on Tony's shoulder.

Tony asked, "Do you have a few hundred dollars on you?"

"I think I do, but I'm not giving you any money until you get some help. I will not stand around and let you destroy yourself."

"I don't have any money!" Tony yelled.

"And you don't need any," replied Bill in a calm voice.

Tony got angry and yelled again, "Fuck you!"

"I know you hate me, but I love you and what I'm doing is for your own good, you will thank me later."

"Thank you for what? Turning your back on me."

"Call me when you're ready to change your life."

"Fuck you! Dick wipe!" Tony yelled.

"I love you, Son," said Bill.

"You're making my life hell."

"You're making your own life hell; I'm just trying to make you understand that your life is more important than those drugs you are living for. Once you realize it, you'll be able to move forward and you will stop. I have never used drugs even when I was in the war, I did not mess with it. It does not add to your life; it takes from it. Learn from your mistakes Son, I will talk to you later," Bill said and got into his car and went home.

Tony remained there at the bus stop thinking how his life became a mess and began to walk to Renay's house. On the way home, Bill thought about Tony if he had given him the money he would have wasted it on drugs digging himself deeper in a hole. *"I will be there for my Son," Bill thought to himself, "I want my Son to bury me, I don't want to bury my Son.*

LESSON 14

True Love Can Never Be Destroyed,
Neither Can You Take from It

Tony arrived at Renay's apartment after that long talk with his father about money and his life, and which he was missing both his money and his life. It was 5pm when Tony got in. Renay was watching TV, her mother was passed out from a drunken stupor.

Renay asked, "Where have you been? Some lady came here looking for you. I think it was your old girlfriend, she said her name was Jennifer. Oh, by the way, she called me a Whore and of course I slapped the Taste Out Her Mouth. She won't be coming by here talking all that Jazz."

"You leave her alone," Tony said.

"She came to my house and disrespected me."

"So, what are you talking about? I did nothing to her."

"She is a good friend of mine," Tony said.

"She told me to tell you she loves you and she is still waiting for you," Renay replied.

"Is that so?" Tony answered.

"Yeah, that's so; also, our son needs some Pampers, talk about that."

"I'll get some when I come back from my mother's house; I'm going to move back to my old apartment," Tony said.

"I don't care where you move, you're going to take care of your son," said Renay.

"I will take care of you also, but I have to go away for a while. I want to get my life back. I want to go back to work, I want to take care of my son the right way," he said.

"Where do I fit in this plan?" Renay asked.

"I may not always be here, but I will send money to you."

"That will be fine," she replied.

"Before I come back, I want you and your mother to stop getting high. And I will get you both nice paying jobs. A better life for you and my son. I can't help you if I can't help myself. I'm tired of living like a nobody and you're somebody too, Renay," he said.

"I know. I just have to pray more and believe in myself. I want to do better," she said, "I don't always want to use drugs, they don't help; besides I could get killed out there."

Renay's mother comes in the room, "I heard you two talking, you two can make it," her mother said, "just do it."

"And we can," they both said.

Fran finally went down to the police station to turn herself in; Betty went with her and so did her Lawyer Tom Simmons.

She spoke to the policeman at the front desk; she spoke softly and said, "My name is Fran Smith, I would like to turn myself in for the murder of Neno Perez."

"Is that so?" the policeman said, "we've been looking for you." He told Fran to step inside a little room where he handcuffed her.

"You have the right to remain silent, anything you say can and will be used against you. If you don't have a lawyer…"

She interrupted him saying, "My lawyer is here with me."

Mr. Simmons introduced himself as her attorney and he would represent her and upcoming court proceedings. Fran was booked on second-degree murder and was given bail. She was released on $500,000.

Bill called Fran on the phone and told her he saw her on TV. *"The news reporter said that the killer of the male escort that was murdered in the motel room last week has been caught and her name was Francine Smith. She is the ex-wife of the CEO of Dark Water Oils Company and was released on bail."*

"I told you were crazy. You killed your lover," Bill said, "he couldn't get a Hard-On and you killed him."

Fran said, "You are a sick Son of a Bitch, that's not what happened."

"I don't care what happen; just don't drag my company down with you. This is not good for our family name," Bill said, "also I want to know how you were in a motel room with an HIV-infected drug user?"

"A what!?" Fran said.

"Yeah, your little boyfriend was infected with the Virus, I hope you protected yourself," Bill said.

"No! she thought to herself."

"Did you have sex with him?'

"That's none of your business."

"You're right about that because I won't be coming to you for sex."

"That's nothing new, we never had sex that much anyway and if we did, you couldn't get it up. And I would have to please myself because you would leave me hanging and hot," Fran said.

"I care about you, I still love you I just can't live with you, I don't want to see any harm come to you," he said.

I still have love for you too," Fran replied.

"I know it was times I hated you, but I stuck it out. I want to be friends with you," Bill said, "I want to be able to talk to you and tell you how I'm feeling or if I had a bad day; just be there for each other." Fran was touched and she started crying.

Bill asked, "Are you crying?"

"Yes, I am."

"You big Dope don't cry."

"I can't help it it's been a long time since you said anything heartfelt like that and it's good to hear."

"I want you to do something for me," Bill said, "I want you to get tested."

"I don't think he had anything," she said.

"You don't know until you get tested."

"You're right, I will go today. Thank you."

"Fran, you get on my nerves, but I don't know what I would do without your big mouth."

"I know that's right," she said.

"You take care…can I have some of my money back?" Bill asked.

"Not a chance," Fran said.

"OK bye, I was just checking," he said.

"Take care." And she hung up.

Fran was riding on an emotional rollercoaster after her talk with Bill; she did not know what to do. She would start crying and then she would stop like she did not have a care in the world, but deep inside she was hurting. Who would comfort her in her time of darkness and where will her light come from? And she remembers God and He said He would never leave her nor forsake her. And Fran fell to her knees and said this prayer to God, "Hear my prayer, O' God. I know I don't pray like I need to, but if You find time can You help me through my tough time and I thank You. I know I was not living the way I should. I have been a sinner all my life, but You are my life and I give it all to You. Amen."

Fran felt God's love descending down on her. The hairs on the back of her neck stood up. She had goosebumps all over her body, it was like someone released the pressure off her life, it was a sign of relief that she never felt better. Therefore, she would go and take the HIV test with God behind her.

Fran called Betty to let her know that God had touched her life,

"Betty, I prayed to God today and He let me know that He is with me."

"That's wonderful Fran God will work it out."

"I know," she said, "I also talked to Bill."

"Are you two getting back together?" Betty asked.

"No, we had a long talk and we put the past behind us and we're going to be friends again."

"Maybe you two can smooth some things out," Betty replied.

"I still love him in a funny kind of way."

"I know he still loves you also."

"He does and we can be the best friends now that we're not together. I don't know if we will ever get back together, but if we do, we will have to find that spark again," Fran said.

"What spark?" Betty replied, "you told me that you never loved Bill and it was all about the money."

"I don't feel that way any longer, it's like something inside me wants and needs to love him with all my heart. God is changing me; I can feel it.

"I'm glad you feel that way because I want to tell you I'm sorry for giving you Neno's number. If I did not give you that number, this would not be happening."

"I also would not have found God," Fran said, "but if I get tested and I TEST POSITIVE I will love God anyway. It won't be the end, it will be the beginning of my love and a relationship that will last until the day I die."

"That is the most beautiful thing I have ever heard," Betty said, "I'm so happy for you that you have inner peace in the middle of a storm."

Fran got up the next day, got dressed, ate her breakfast sat down at her table, and thought about the long day ahead of her. *She looked around the room and realized it was empty with Bill gone. She missed him and thought to herself, "I must go on, I can't give up. This is the day that will change my life forever.*

And at that moment, she grabbed her keys, bolted out the door, jumped into her car and went to the doctor's office. She will find out soon enough if she was infected or not.

LESSON 15

Be Not a Part of Those Whose Paths are Crooked
And Who are Devious in Their Ways

It was Tony's first day in the rehab clinic, he was ready to get his life in order. He entered the clinic right after he spoke to Renay. He thought of her and their son and how she had stopped using drugs.

Jennifer dropped by to see how he was doing. She told Tony that she still loves him and wanted to work things out between them.

"I love you too," Tony said.

"What about the other woman?"

"What about her?" Tony replied, "she is just the mother of my son."

"Do you still want to be with her?" Jennifer asked.

"Not like that," Tony replied, "we are just going to be friends."

"I like the sound of that," Jennifer said, "it's me and you against the world. Sweetheart, how is your mother doing?"

"Fine, I have not talked to her in a few weeks. She has not returned my calls. I have to stop by and see her when I get out of here," Tony said.

"I want us to be a family and maybe one day you'll give me a baby," Jennifer said, "I always wanted a son so when I found out you had a son by another woman I was very angry. That's why I called her a Whore and she socked me good. I had to go home and lay down; I had a bad headache, she slapped the Shit out of me."

"Jennifer, you never could hold your tongue," said Tony.

"She told me the next time I say something smart she'll pull my tongue out," said Jennifer.

"She really is a nice person, you just pushed the wrong button, that's all.

That's why you got slapped."

A VOICE CAME ON THE LOUDSPEAKER: *VISITING HOURS ARE NOW OVER. PLEASE PROCEED TO THE EXIT FOR DEPARTURE.*

"I want you to come back and see me," said Tony.

"You know I will. You don't have to ask me, I love you, Tony. I waited for you through your drug thing and I will wait for you through this also," Jennifer said.

THE VOICE CAME ON AGAIN*: VISITING HOURS ARE NOW OVER PLEASE PROCEED TO THE EXIT.*

"I think you better go before they take my next visit." He kissed Jennifer gently on the lips and she left. After Tony's visit with Jennifer, he called Bill.

"Hey, Dad."

"What's up Son"

"Nothing much, just getting my life in order."

"That's good Son."

"I will have you back on track in no time," Bill said, "call me the day you get out and we will go celebrate the return of your life."

"That will be fine," Tony said.

"I don't want to take up much of your time, I know you got work to do; so, see you later," said Bill.

"Alright, bye." And they hung up.

Tony thought of his mother and how she was dealing with the fact that she had killed someone and he wondered why she did it. And why was she in a strange man's room, was he mom's lover? I don't know? He thought to himself. I hope she comes out of this alright. I hope she does not go to jail because she's hasn't been in any trouble all her life. She had some tough times growing up and grandad took her through some stuff that she still holds on to and the baggage she carries makes her feel down. I don't think she would survive in prison... Tony was in a daze thinking of his mother and then someone shook his arm, "Mr. Smith, it's dinner time."

"Alright," Tony said.

He went to eat his dinner. It was like a country club for the rich, in fact, it was for the rich. Tony enjoyed himself learning about addiction and it confirms that if we are addicts, we suffer from abuse and hurt our bodies. And we shall remain quiet as we listen to our inner selves telling us to release the beast of addiction.

Tony began to see how addiction wasn't consuming his life and would never cross the bridge again. You can't expect to live a good life and do drugs; the two cannot coexist without chaos and disappointment.

The group that Tony was in talked about how their families wanted the best for them and would not put up with their drug use. Tony stayed in the program for 90 days, enough time to focus on his life and his future. He called Jennifer to come and pick him up. He told her that he loved her and wanted to get their lives back on track.

Tony stopped by Renay's apartments on his way home (Jennifer waited in the car) because he wanted to see his son. He knocked on the door, but nobody came. He knocked again and the door came open so, he stepped in calling for Renay, and then she finally answered.

"Who is it? *(she saw that it was Tony)* How did you get in here?" Renay asked.

"The door was open."

"Well it should have been locked," she said, "and I know you have something for me and your son."

"I do, but I wanted to tell you I can't see you anymore I'm getting married," Tony said.

"Congratulations, I'm happy for you, but that does not change the fact that you have a son. I don't care about that; what I do care about is you taking care of your son."

"I will take care of my son."

"You do that," she said.

"Where is my son?"

"He's not here."

"Where is he?

"My mother has him; she took him with her to the store."

"Where at?"

"I don't know," Renay said.

"Are you sure she did not take him to some crack house?"

"My mother does not use anymore."

"That's good," he said, "I'm going to write you a check for $2,000 that should hold you for a few weeks."

"Thank you, you're a good father and a good friend; your son is lucky he has you and so am I. Thank you for coming in my life. I know we went through some hard times together, but look at us now, God is good," Renay said, "I know it was strange how we met. I was lonely in my life being a dancer coming home to no one to love, but I thank you for my son, he made my life worth living. God sent you to me to change my life and to make me a better person."

She began to cry because her life was changing before her eyes; she was free from drugs and happiness was hers.

Renay went on to say, "When I was in my drug activity I used manipulation and domination which influences my behavior for people, places, and things. Which I used through my body and my feelings. Which disturbs my soul and causes my will to be weakened, my mind to be dark and in my emotions to be unbalanced. And I look to God to free me from my foolishness, stay clean and take it one day at a time."

And Tony said, "I see you have been learning."

"I go to NA, it's called Narcotics Anonymous; I'm in a 12-step program; I've become the Renay God meant me to be *(then she said to Jennifer who was sitting in the car)* I'm sorry for slapping you."

She replied, "I'm sorry too. Also, I should not have acted that way."

"I forgive you."

"Can we be friends?" Jennifer asked.

"Sure, we can," Renay quickly answered.

Then Tony said, "I have to go, I'll call you later."

Jennifer said to Renay, "We'll talk; maybe we can go shopping and get to know each other."

"Sounds good, I will let you know, it will be soon; maybe later this week," Renay replied.

Renay felt good; she was clean, her baby's father was rich and one day her son would be. Also, he would take care of his mother.

At that moment, her mother walked in with her son and Renay said jokingly, "Grandma kidnapped you?" *(talking to her son as she grabs him from her mother and hugged and kissed him)* "mommy loves her Baby.

And Mark smiles softly and said, "Mom-Mom." Those were his first words, and they hugged each other as Renay held the baby.

Renay forgot she had a man in her room before Tony came. He never came out while Tony was there. Before Renay came out she told her date not to move and don't come out of the room.

"I don't want you to mess me up with my baby's daddy. He has it going on, he has money; he's not like your Broke Ass," she told him, "as a matter of fact, after he leaves you take your no giving rent Ass back to your mothers."

A few minutes later Renay returned to the room, "I told you I want you to leave."

"But we just had sex."

"So, what?" she replied.

"But I love you,"

"Man, carry your Ass on; I don't want you anymore," Renay said.

"I don't have anywhere to go!" he replied in an angry voice.

"I don't care where you go, but you're getting out of here; even if I have to call the police."

"So, you're gonna to do me like that? I gave you all my money," he said.

"You're right! You gave it to me and I did not take it."

"Please don't do this to me! I have no money! I have nowhere to go!" he said. And then he started getting louder.

"My son is asleep, stop making all this noise," Renay said in a soft tone.

"Well, can I have some of my money back?"

"I'm not giving you anything," she said with a stern voice.

At that moment, he went berserk. He grabbed his knife out of his coat and started stabbing Renay. She screamed for her mother who left out for a moment. He stabbed Renay 40 times. As she lays dying on the floor, he takes the money that he gave her for her son and then runs out of the door. Her son crawls into the room to his mother whose life has expired. As he grabs for her he gets blood all over himself. Renay's mother finally comes in and finds her dead.

She screams, "RENAY!!!!! NOOOO!!! SOMEBODY CALL THE POLICE!!!" But no one could save her; she was gone.

Renay Benson dead at 25.

LESSON 16

A Gracious Woman Retains Her Honor
And a Strong Man Retains Wealth

The traffic was terrible as she left to go to the doctor's office. She arrived about 3 o'clock. She was very nervous and scared, but she knew God would help her through whatever is coming down the pike.

Dr. Brenda Stevens came in the office, "Hello Mrs. Smith how are you feeling today? Fine, I hope."

"I'm alright I guess, I'm a little nervous," Fran said.

"That's understandable," Dr. Stevens replied, "I will be taking some blood."

"Alright, that will be fine," Fran said.

Dr. Stevens proceeded to take her blood, "This won't hurt a bit," the doctor said. Then she pierced her skin.

"You're done already?"

"Yes," said Dr. Stevens.

"You're good."

"It will take about two weeks for your results."

"I have to wait that long?" Fran asked.

"Yes, but I think I can work something out to get your test results back in a week. Your test will be sent with an urgent request so, it will come this Friday around noon. That's when the mail truck comes," the doctor said.

"That's fine," Fran said.

For the whole week, Fran was on pins and needles, she was eating a lot of junk food to calm her nerves; soda, chips, cake, ice cream and getting fat.

And she wanted to anyway because if she tested positive, she did not want to lose weight like the people she saw at the doctor's office and in the HIV literature she read.

The 5 days passed and Fran arrived at 1pm at the doctor's office, she went to the front desk; the receptionist asked, "May I help you?"

Fran answered, "Yes. My name is Francine Smith I'm here to see Dr. Brenda Stevens."

"One moment please, you can have a seat," she said.

"Thank you," Fran replied.

Dr. Stevens came to the waiting room to get Fran, "May I speak to you?"

"Yes," she said.

"Walk this way."

Fran noticed the living with AIDS Journals in Brenda's office *"This will be the moment of truth," she thought to herself as she sat down in a two-chair office.*

The doctor said to Fran, "I have your results."

"And what are they?"

Dr. Stevens is hesitating in telling Fran the results, therefore she becomes angry, "Will you give me the Damn results!"

"Oh yes, of course, you have tested positive for the virus that causes AIDS." Fran dropped her head and weeps softly.

"Are you alright?" the doctor asked.

"No, I'm not, I just received the most devastating news I have ever heard next to losing my mother, but I'm not letting this thing kill me. Tell me about this disease and how does it work."

Dr. Stevens responded, "Scientists have long understood the natural history of the HIV infection which has not changed since the first reports of AIDS in 1981.

"So, this is fairly new?" Fran asked.

"Yes," the doctor replied, "on an average, a decade passes from the time of infection to the time of death. Some people have died within 1 to 2 years of infection. I will be starting you on a treatment plan, but as I was saying people have died within 1 to 2 years of the infection, others will die 15 to 20 years after being infected; it's bell-shaped, but again less than 5% of people will survive their HIV infection if untreated. There are people who believe that because they are HIV negative despite unsafe sexual behavior they are somehow immune to HIV. We do not yet have a test to identify with an innate resistance to the disease. One person can have a single sex encounter and get infected or a hundred and not get infected. Sooner or later the vast majority of those playing Russian Roulette with the virus will get infected," then Dr. Stevens stopped her explanation and asked, "how do you think you got infected?"

"Sex," she replied.

"With whom?"

"A friend."

"You have to contact him to let him know he may have been exposed to the virus. Therefore, he also needs to be tested," the doctor said.

"He can't be notified," Fran said.

"Why not?"

"Because I killed him?"

"You killed him? Why?"

"Because we had unprotected sex and then he told me he was an intravenous drug user."

"I see," she said, "I want to set up an appointment to start your treatment regimen.

"What's out there as far as treatment medications?" Fran asked.

"There is a drug called AZT, you have to take one 400 mg pill every 4 hours around the clock. It has some adverse side effects; headaches, nausea, and vomiting, for every patient the side effects are different," the doctor said, "but I want to see you next week and try some medications to see what works."

"Alright, that will be fine," Fran said.

"You're going to be alright," Dr. Steven said as she looked Fran straight in the eyes trying to reach her soul with her kind words of encouragement.

"I will be okay, God has my back."

"That's good, then I'll see you next week."

"Next week," Fran repeated, "I'll see you then." Fran walked away with her head high thinking HIV is not going to kill her.

When Fran got home she called Betty.

Betty answered the phone, "Hello."

"Guess who?"

"Oh, Fran is that you?

"Sure is," she said, "I just came back from the doctor."

"What happened," Betty asked.

"I have it the virus that causes AIDS," she said as she started to cry and Betty also started crying.

This was truly a dark day for both women it was like the world ended, but Fran would truly start living from this tragedy. Betty with tears in her eyes feeling her friends pain said, "This is not the end, this is where your happy ending begins and you are going to win."

"Thank you for being my friend."

"It's nothing, that's what friends are for," Betty replied to Fran.

"I love you, Friend."

"I love you too Girl," Betty said, "hey let's go shopping and spend lots of money."

"Sure, why not, you only live once," said Fran.

"You got that right. I will be there to pick you up."

"Okay, see you when you get here," Fran said.

LESSON 17

Hatred Stirs up Strife, but Love Covers All Wrongs

Tony and Jennifer arrived at Tony's high rise apartment; after shopping and spending time together after stopping by Renay's. As soon as he got in he wanted to call Renay's because he had a funny feeling that something was wrong. He called Renay's apartment but got no answer. He kept on calling, but no one would pick up. Therefore, he decided he would try later.

Tony and Jennifer sat down to watch TV after dinner, he asked Jennifer to hand him the remote control.

"I want to watch some news," he said to her and changed the channel to it. It was just coming on.

The Newsman reported that "A woman was found dead in an apartment in upper east side of New York today, the victim's name is being withheld until relatives can be notified. The woman's son was inside when the attack happened. The boy was not hurt; the girls' mother was just returning from the store when she found her daughter in a pool of blood; also, the baby is in the care of family members. No suspects have been found. If you have any information concerning this crime, please call the police. Tony said to himself, I hope that's not Renay.

Jennifer said, "I think it's Renay, we just left her."

"No, it's not her," Tony said.

The phone rang about 3pm the next day and it was Renay's mother calling.

Jennifer answered the phone, "Hello."

"Is Tony there? It's very urgent that I speak with him," replied Renay's mother.

"Hold on…Tony telephone."

Tony took the phone, "Hello."

"Tony, it's Renay's mother, Renay's dead."

"She's what?"

"She was stabbed to death by her boyfriend."

"When," he asked.

"Yesterday."

"So, that was her on the news."

"Yes."

"Where's my son?"

"I have him with me," she said, "I have no money to bury her, she did not have any Life Insurance before she died."

"I'll take care of it," Tony said.

"Thank you," Renay's mother said.

"I will miss her very much, she made me see how important my life was and I'm grateful to her," Tony said, "it will take a long time to replace the friendship we had. Jennifer and I have a good friendship, but Renay and I had that something that made me see that life was not always peaches and cream. And all that I have can be taken in a New York minute and I could be living on the street."

"Speaking of the street, what will you be doing with Renay's apartment?" Renay's mother asked.

"Well, I was thinking that you could stay there," he said.

"But I'm not working, I won't be able to pay rent," she said.

"I will pay your rent for a year while you get yourself together. You'll be starting your new job too. I told you before I left that when I came back I would take care of you if you stayed clean. You have held your part of the bargain and I will hold mine."

She became excited and said, "Thank you!" She repeated 3 times as she started to cry realizing that Renay would not be there to share in her happiness. Renay's tragic death became a blessing for her mother; one life lost and one saved. She will be able to look at her grandson and remember her beautiful daughter.

Tony said, "I will take care of everything, you get some rest and I will call you tomorrow."

"Alright," she said.

"Bye now, you're going to be alright," he said and hangs up.

Jennifer is looking at him with his head hanging down.

"What's wrong?" Jennifer asked.

"Renay's dead," he replied as he begins to weep; Jennifer hugs him and tells him don't cry, but he loved Renay and she is gone. *He thought of his son and how would he react to not seeing his mother; only time will tell.*

John Blackson returned to his mother's house after he murdered Renay Benson; he knocks on the door.

His mother comes to the door and asked, "What do you want?"

"I want to talk to you," he said.

"What about?" she asked as she sees blood all over his shirt, "who have you been fighting?" The chain lock is on the door so, he is talking to his mother through a crack in the door.

"You are not coming in here; I saw your girlfriend on the news; somebody killed her."

"I didn't do it," he said.

"You're going to have a hard time convincing me with all that blood on you; go to turn yourself in," she said.

"Are you crazy, I'm a have court in the streets," he said.

"Well, in the meantime, you should go hide somewhere."

"Let me hide here."

"Have you lost your mind? So, they can tear my house apart looking for you. I love you, you're my son, but I can't help you. You have done a very bad thing," she said, "go turn yourself in and I will send you some money to take care of your personal needs. I love you, but you have to get away from my door before the police think you're here and kick it in."

He begs for her to open the door and she said, "Wait, I'll be right back." He sits on the steps.

"You hungry?" she asked.

"Yes, I am." She closes the door, gets the phone to call the police.

"Police or ambulance?" the dispatcher asked.

"Police," John's mother said.

"What's the problem?"

"I know who killed that girl."

"Who?"

"My son."

"Where is he now?"

"He's at my house."

"Where do you live?"

"316 Bertha Parker Lane."

"We will send someone out," said the dispatcher.

"Thank you." John's mother returns to the door with something to eat to stall him until the police come. Five minutes later he hears the police sirens in the distance.

He looks at his mother and said, "You Fuckin Bitch You Set Me Up!"

"It's for your own good," she said.

"What's good about me going to prison?"

"I don't want you to get hurt," she said as she started to cry because she hated to do what she had done. John's pulls out his knife at the police. He's waving the knife; the police have 9 guns pointed at him.

"Drop your weapon," the police said.

"You're going to have to kill me, I'm not dropping nothing," he said as he looks at his mother, "see what you made me do. I have Renay's blood on my hands and now you have mine on yours." And he rushes toward the police who opens fire killing him.

His mother said nothing as her son drops to the ground. She screams at the police you're going to kill him. She finally comes out and drops to her knees to help her son.

"He's dying," and she said while looking at her son, "I'm sorry John."

"Fuck You Bitch!" he yells as blood comes from his mouth. And immediately then he dies in her arms. The police grabbed her and pulled her away from her dead son.

"You did not have to kill him!" she yelled.

"He attacked us with the knife; we had no choice, but to open fire. I'm sorry," the police said, "I hate when we are forced to take a life. You made the call so, you'll have to live with that."

"I did not want you people to kill him!" she cried.

LESSON 18

Do Not Withhold Good from Those Whom it is Due, When It is in Your Power to Do So

Tony made all the arrangements and paid for his friend Renay's funeral. The people she worked with came to pay their respects to a good person who took the wrong path in life. It's sad that she lived so fast and died so young. Tony hoped that a lot of young people would see her life as a lesson and not as a tragedy.

It saddened Tony that she was gone, he felt he could have made a difference in her life if she had lived. *"This young lady did not even get a chance to live. All the work she had to do will go undone, all the dreams she had will go unrealized, and all the children she would have had will never be born. But now, it's all over,"* Tony thought to himself.

<u>The Confessions:</u>

Fran called Bill the next day after she received her results from her HIV test. She hoped he would still be her friend even though she has tested positive.

Bill answered, "Hello."

"Bill is that you?"

"It is I My Sweet," he said.

"Bill, what are you doing with yourself these days Lover Boy? Are you still getting in the shower with all your clothes on and wishing Charlie would come and put you out of your misery?"

"Nah, he said, "I was waiting for you to call me and tell me the status of your test and where do we go from here."

"I have bad news," she said, "I tested POSITIVE."

"Oh Fran," he replied.

"But I'm going to be alright, God is with me and He won't let me go through this alone," she said.

"You are so right and I'm with you also," Bill said, "I know we went through a lot of problems throughout the years, but let's put all that behind us; because if we stay in the past we will have no future. I loved you, the first time I saw you and I still do. I will love you more because you need that right now. We will fight your disease together."

Fran replied, "I have to admit, sometimes I don't think I love you like you love me, but I've learned to love you. I'm sorry I hurt you, if I did not fool around on you I will not be HIV Positive which might be a death sentence. But God will pardon me from that. I have learned that I can't take life for granted anymore and cherish what life I have left."

"I want to ask you something? I would like to ask you on a date," Bill said.

"I don't know…I'm so busy doing nothing. Of course, I will go on a date with you Old Friend. And we are friends so, don't think you gonna get any," she said jokingly.

"I will wait until our 3rd date," Bill said. He was making Fran feel good; that he was not treating her different because of her condition and she knew it.

"I want to say that you have lifted my spirits. I don't feel down, I don't feel alone, and I don't feel abandoned. I thank God for you," she said.

"I thank God for you also, even though you're a Pain in The You Know What."

"Sorry, love me anyway," she said.

He replied, "I will...I meant to ask you, have you spoken to Tony?"

"Yes," she answered.

"I heard his baby's mother was murdered last week in her apartment. And how is our grandson?" Bill asked.

"Oh, he is fine. He's staying with family on his mother's side. Oh, that poor girl, she was really a nice person," Fran said.

"I hope you're alright," he said.

"I'm fine," she replied. Fran let Bill go and hangs up the phone because she wanted to go to an HIV Support Group to find out more about the disease.

Then Fran thought to herself, "I won't let this get me down. I'm in to win it."

LESSON 19

He that Makes Himself Rich Yet, He Has Nothing
He that Makes Himself Poor Yet, He Has Everything

Tony went to get his son from Renay's mother who has started a new life and has a job. Tony will raise his son, along with Jennifer and Renay's mother helping when she can. They were becoming a real family. Tony wanted to make everything complete. Therefore, he and Jennifer were engaged a year after Renay's death.

Mark was 2-years-old and he was a cute little boy. He will grow up to be a handsome young man and with his silver spoon; he will have no money problems. Tony will tell him how wonderful his mother was and how she loved him. Also, she would do whatever it took to make sure he was alright.

Renay gave him life and lost hers, a hard lesson in which she will never recover from.

LESSON 20

Live Your Life Today Like You Will Die Tomorrow
And the Fullness of It

The day came when the entire family got together; Bill, Fran, Tony, Jennifer, Little Mark, and Ronda Benson (Renay's Mother). Ronda became a special part of the family; it was like her life started over. She was happy for the first time in a long time, but something was missing. What was missing was Renay, a space that will be empty forever, but she will live in their hearts and a day will not go by without thinking of her. We can thank Mark for that because he is a splitting image of his mother.

Bill and Fran got married again, as a matter of fact, Tony and Jennifer got married the same day Bill and Fran did, so it was a double wedding with all the trimmings. Fran started living instead of dying.

Bill said to Fran, "I will love you as long as I live."

"And I will do the same," she replied.

They all decided to go to Renay's grave to have a picnic and remember the good times; also, to plan the future. For life, will only give you what you ask for and that's a fact.

The day came when Fran went to court, Bill was in the courtroom supporting his wife. She was charged with First Degree Murder. She was facing life in prison, but her lawyer said Fran would not get any jail time. Betty was paying Mr. Simmons $20,000 for taking Fran's case. The State offered Fran 5 years in jail to take a plea. She refused and chose to go to trial and fight the State.

The prosecution presented evidence that Fran planned to kill Neno because he used drugs, that's why she had a bat in her car and thought no one would find out. And she thought her social status would keep her out of jail for the murder of a nobody drug user, who Fran used for sex and their relationship lasted for 6 months.

It took the State a year to bring Fran to trial; her jury was made up of 8 women and 4 men. During the jury selection, Mr. Simmons said that she was very wise in choosing 8 women and 4 men because the women would take her side and lower the charges to a lesser count.

Mr. Simmons presented evidence that Fran attacked Neno out of rage and did not plan his murder. He would have to put Fran on the stand concerning their relationship and that Fran paid Neno for sex. He would also have to explain to the jury that Neno had unprotected sex with Fran knowing he was infected with HIV. He would also tell the jury that the bat in her car was her son's Tony and not for killing someone. That's why it was in a box. He would also tell them that Neno gave Fran a death sentence when he had sex with her. Bill, Tony, and Jennifer sat right behind Fran's table in the courtroom. Mr. Simmons told the jury that Fran did in fact murder Neno Perez and if he was still alive he would be charged with attempted murder for giving Fran Acquired Immune Deficiency Syndrome and her life will never be the same. He told the jury that Neno was a victim of a crime and my client is also a victim of a crime. She must take one 400mg pill every 4 hours' night and day; a punishing schedule for this poor woman. She also goes through significant adverse side effects such as headaches, nausea, and vomiting to name a few.

After presenting the evidence Mr. Simmons then pleaded to the jury, "So you tell me who the real victim is? My heart goes out to the Perez

Family for his death, but my client has to live with this disease every day for the rest of her life. That's why it's your job to find her not guilty of First Degree Murder. So, that she may return to her family to live the rest of her life in peace. You cannot sentence this woman a second time. She is already on death row for HIV and to put this woman in prison, she would surely die. So, I ask you men and women of the jury, please help this woman Francine Smith regain some part of her life. Thank you."

Fran was pleased with her lawyer. *"The $20,000 put up for my defense was well spent," she thought to herself.*

Next, the Prosecution presented its case.

The Prosecution said, "You have a woman who claims she is a victim. She may be a victim, but I ask you, was she a victim, before the murder or after it? That is something you should think about when you find her guilty or not. I have read her medical documents and she has been infected with the virus. My heart goes out to the Smith Family as well as Francine Smith. I'm truly saddened by this information *(he looks directly at Fran)* I'm very sorry. But I have a job to do and that job is to convince you that Francine Smith is a murder. You might have heard someone say that Mrs. Smith killed Neno Perez because he infected her with the virus. Mr. Perez did, in fact, infect her with the virus, but when? That is the question we must ask ourselves. Neno Perez was killed on October 13, 1986; Fran Smith found out she was infected October 26, 1986. So, she did not know if she was infected until that date. Therefore, she killed him because he had unprotected sex with her and used drugs. This is a woman who has it all; money, power and prestige who just wanted to pay for sex and go home to her family. But what I want to say is that she forgot a few things and that was loyalty, ladies and gentlemen of the jury. Another thing she forgot was to protect herself during sex. She would have never been infected if he wore a condom. She has herself to blame for her condition, not Neno Perez who is dead because she assumed he had a disease. I want to ask you, good people of the jury, let's pretend that Neno Perez did not have the virus at the time of his death, but the killing part remains the same. Lady and gents, Francine Smith is a murderer with the virus or without it. She killed in cold blood, therefore she must pay. I leave you with this as you go and make your decision. Remember, there will be no winners in this case; a man is dead and a woman is scarred for life. I leave you to your work, decide wisely thank you," the Prosecution rest Your Honor.

The Judge asked the Defense, "Would there be anything more Mr. Simmons."

"The Defense rest also."

"The jury may go deliberate," the Judge instructed.

It took the jury 12 hours to come to a decision. She was found guilty of murder, but of a lesser charge of Manslaughter. She received 5 years in prison. Fran felt good that all she got was 5 years because she could have gotten life in prison.

She hugged Mr. Simmons, Bill, Tony, and Jennifer. She was happy, but she forgot what was lurking in her blood stream. A lesson well learned.

LESSON 21

Those You See Going Up
Will Be the Same One's You See Coming Down

It was 1987 when Fran started her sentence of 5 years at Silent Hill Prison. And she was upbeat about it, considering the fact she could have gotten more than 5 years in jail.

The Warden wanted to speak to Fran after she was photographed. Fran was home for 6 months before she was to report to prison to serve her sentence. The Warden's name was Jake Swells, who had just started the job because the previous Warden was fired for having sex with inmates. This new Warden would change things; so, everyone hoped. But Mr. Swells sent for Fran. She entered his office with two guards beside her.

"Hello, Mrs. Freeman. How are you doing today?" Then he instructed her to have a seat. Then she sat down.

"The reason I wanted to see is because I would like to know where you would like to be housed?" he asked.

Fran answered, "What do you mean?"

"I asking you if you want protected custody or regular population."

"What's the difference?" she asked.

"Well with protective custody you will be locked up most in time for your own protection in a cell by yourself. And in regular popular, you will be treated like every other inmate and I can't guarantee your safety."

"I don't want to be locked up by myself all the time, I'm gonna take my chances in population. I would really go crazy if I don't have someone to talk to."

"I think that settles that," Mr. Swells said, "I want her sent to Cell Block

C; those girls there are model inmates so, she should be alright."

"Thank you, Sir," Fran said.

"It's my pleasure and it's my job to make sure you make it out of here alive."

The guard then asked Fran, "Are you ready to go and is it anything else you want to know before we leave?"

"No," she answers.

"Alright then let's go."

Fran stood up to appraise the situation that she was in. She was a little bit scared. *"But I'll be alright," she thought to herself.*

Fran was then given a blue uniform with the letters D.O.C which stands for the Department of Corrections, two sheets, a blanket, a bar of soap and toothbrush.

Then Fran asked the guard, "Is this all I get?"

"Yes, it is, this is not the Holiday Inn so don't get it confused Miss Money Bags. Nobody here is gonna serve you Caviar, Lobster or any of that Shit. The closest thing you'll get to seafood is a Fish Sticks. All we have here is good old State slop. Get used to it," the guard said, "oh I forgot we do serve tuna fish; we do serve that."

Fran was then taken to Cell Block C. As she entered women were yelling, "New Meat! New Meat!" Some of these women were beautiful with their hair in all types of styles. The guard told Fran to go Cell 20, top bunk. A couple of women followed Fran to her cell.

One of the women said, "I know you, you were on TV for killing that Spanish guy."

Fran looked at the women and said, "Yes, that was me."

"How are you doing? I'm Verna your cell mate."

Fran said, "Hi, nice to meet you."

"Same here," Verna said.

"I want to know how is it in here?" Fran asked.

"Well, let me put it to you this way; you can't go when you want, can't eat when you want unless you have some commissary."

"What's that?" she asked.

"The stuff you buy at the store; to answer your question, I'd rather be anywhere but here."

"That bad huh?"

"Worst on holidays because you miss family, friends and good food." And then a woman peeked in the door and asked, "Who's the New Meat?"

"Fran," as she answers with a venomous expression.

"My name is Gina, I run this block. If you need anything let me know. I mean anything," as she licked her lips.

"I need something."

"What," Gina answered.

"I need you to stay out of my face Lena, or Gina, whatever your name is."

"Oh, it's like that?"

"It's like that," Fran said.

"I like that playing hard to get. I think I'm in love with you," Gina said licking her lips again.

"I know you better do something with that tongue before you lose it."

"I want to lose it in you." Then suddenly Verna slams the door.

"That Bitch is Crazy."

"That she is," Fran responded.

Gina was beautiful light-skinned Black girl who could have been a model if she didn't do the crime that got her in prison. Gina killed her boyfriend in a jealous rage one night after a party. Her boyfriend Mike West was seeing her and another girl and she caught them in the bathroom when they thought Gina was sleeping and drunk. What Mike didn't know is that Gina was awake the entire time. She walked behind Mike and his friend. She and Mike were to be married in a few weeks and now she was heartbroken. As placed her ear on the door, the tears began to flow down her face. Then she lifted her ear from the door and tiptoed downstairs and opened the knife drawer and took out a Butcher's knife and walked slowly back up the steps. As she approached the door she could hear sounds of passion and then she kicked the door open.

She yelled, "What the hell is going on here!?" with the knife in her hand, "I'm going to kill you and this Bitch."

Mike begins to beg, "I can explain."

"Then explain to me why you're in the bathroom with another woman with your pants down."

"I was trying talk to her," he said.

"Now you're playing me stupid?" she asked him scarastically as she begins to cut him on the hands as he tries to stop the attack."

The woman managed to grab the knife by the blade cutting her hand. But in the long run, it would save her life. They fought for a few minutes as Mike laid in the hallway bleeding to death. The bathroom had an arresting scent of semen and blood.

The knife is then grabbed by the women's brother who pulled the two apart and then asked, "What happened here?"

"Call the cops, this Bitch is tried to kill me," the women screamed as she tended to Mike trying to stop the bleeding.

Mike died at the hospital because he lost too much blood. Gina was then arrested and was given a ten-year prison sentence.

"I'm gonna have to watch that Homo Bitch," Fran said, "Verna did she ever give you any trouble while you were here?"

"She sure did."

"What did she do to you?"

"She gave me a lot of friendship."

"What do you mean by that?"

"She took care of me when I didn't have anything."

"That's not trouble; looks like you found a friend."

"But she wanted to have sex with me," Verna replied, "but I thought I owed her something so I let her go downtown so-to-speak."

"I can't believe you felt for that if you need anything crap. She wheeled you in; hook line and sinker."

"I smelled her a mile away. That's why I told her to stay out of my face. I knew she was up to something. So, Verna, how did you end up in this Shit Hole?"

"I'm here on an attempted murder charge."

"How did that happened?"

"My boyfriend and I were getting high on Speed, drinking and having sex on this night. I was so high I did not know what I was doing. The next thing I knew; I was in a police car. I did not know how I got there so I asked the cop what did I do? He said I beat up a midget."

Fran laughed at that part of the story and said, "I'm sorry, finish the rest of it."

"I beat the little guy with a beer bottle and pushed him in front of a car."

"How tall are you?"

"5'7"

"And how tall was the midget?"

"I don't remember. The cops said he was real short."

"I bet that was funny. So how much time did you get for that?"

"Seven years."

"I don't need to tell you how I got here. You know the whole story."

"Just the part about you killing Neno Perez. You know he has a sister here."

"He does?" Fran said.

"Yes, he does," she quickly replied, "she's on another cell block. I think if she reads the paper, she knows you'll here." At that moment, Fran felt shivers run up her spine. *Thinking to herself, "She may have to confront this woman and may have to show some ferocity. Then she might leave her alone."*

Verna looked into Fran eye's and she could see and smell fear. "You not scared, are you?"

"Maybe just a little. What's her name?"

"Her name is Joyce. She's a pretty nice person."

"What is she here for?"

"She had some girl beat up for owing her money. She does not have a lot of time. She gets out next year on 2 years. So, you might be the last thing on her mind. She wants to go home to her kids; she has 3 sons."

"I have a son also," Fran said, "what about you Verna, you have kids?"

"No," she answered.

"Do you want any?"

"Sure, if the right man along. I would give him all the kids he wants."

"How old are you?" Fran asked.

"27."

"You're too young to be sitting here. When do you get out?"

"In 3 years."

"That's not long."

"If I get good time or I make parole, I'll get out next year."

"I wanna make parole," Fran said.

"I hope you do. Maybe I can hang out with you."

"I don't know. I would have to get to know you better."

"Better how?" Verna asked.

"Not like that. I don't like women. Don't put that in your empty head."

"Who you calling an empty head?"

"I didn't mean it like that. I meant keep your mind empty of thoughts like that. I'm gonna lie down for a few hours before dinner. Wake me up when it's time to eat. Okay, Verna?"

"Sure."

"I have to get some rest," Fran thought to herself as she climbed up the latter on her bunk bed. "I'm gonna get that bottom bunk, even if I have to pay for it." And drifted she off to sleep in that strange place that would be her home for the next 5 years.

The chow hall line was long as Fran waited her turn to be served. For dinner, they had fish that was dry, beans that didn't have any taste, cornbread that was hard, and Jell-O that looked like water.

Fran asked Verna when she sat down, "How can you eat this slop?"

"I don't have a lot of money so I have to eat what's on this tray or I'll starve. I know you'll gonna eat good."

"I have to get to that canteen first," Fran said.

"I'll teach you how to make meals out of tuna fish and cup of soups. If you don't like this food buy your own, some people never eat this mess."

"I see why," Fran said, "I'm not gonna eat this if I can help it."

Fran looks at Verna eating and said, "I see you don't play; you eat everything on your tray."

"That's right, and if you don't want yours, hand it over," Verna said looking at Fran's tray.

"I'm gonna eat the fish, but you can have the rest of it. I see why your fat, you're a Human Trashcan."

"So, what you're jealous because you don't have a body like this?" she asked and then she stands up and runs her hand down her thigh, "I might have picked up a few pounds, but I can still DROP IT LIKE IT'S HOT."

"I don't want to drop anything," Fran replied.

"You don't have much to drop with your Flat Ass," Verna said as she grabbed Fran's fish off her tray.

"You can have that," she said with sarcasm in her voice. Then Fran took her tray to the window to be cleaned. Verna picked up her tray also following behind Fran.

"Wait up Bitch."

Fran turned around and said, "Who you calling a Bitch."

Verna immediately put her hands up, "I didn't mean nothing by saying that. That's how we talk to each other. Take it easy, it's cool Celli."

"I'm sorry, but I don't like to be called a Bitch. These women may not mine, but I do. My mother did name me Bitch so don't call me one. Fran is my name. Do you want me to spell it for you?"

"Alright, I'm sorry."

"Don't be sorry, be careful!" As Fran turned to go back to her cell block.

Verna felt real stupid for talking to Fran like that. She forgot that Fran was a millionaire that so happened to be her roommate. Then a light came on in Verna's head; if she's playing her cards right, Fran would take care of her and she could have all the Little Debby Cakes she wants. All she has to do is don't let her mouth get her in where she doesn't fit in.

The entire time Verna and Fran are talking Gina not far behind ease dropping to find out anything she can. Gina walked on the block right after the two women did.

Gina said to Fran, "You good in your prison uniform." As she throws her a kiss. But Fran ignored her and went in her cell.

"I think she likes you, Ms. Fran," Verna said.

"I don't like her; I'm not that way. She might float your boat, but not mine. I have a husband; I don't need a fake wife. I don't know how you can live with yourself after you let that women touch you."

"I don't think about it. It happened and there is nothing I can do to take it back. Besides, I loved it…and I'll do it again," said Verna.

"Your one Sick Puppy; you know that?" Fran replied.

"I guess she likes White Meat and I got it for her," Verna said.

"I don't know what you're talking about, but you're Crazy," Fran said as she sat on Verna's bunk, "oh, I was meaning to ask you, what would it cost me to trade bunks with you?" As she looked at Verna and feeling how soft it was. "This is nice and low to the ground."

"I don't know, just look out for me when you eat. When you eat, I wanna eat and when you drink, I wanna drink."

"Oh, My God, you're Greedy. Do you ever get enough to eat? It's a deal. I like to eat too; so, they may be rolling us both out of here when we leave." And they laughed until someone knocked on the door. It was Karen Nelson one of Verna's friends asking if she wanted to play cards with them.

"Not really," said Verna.

"Come on please!" Then she asked Fran if she wanted to play.

"What are they playing?" Fran asked.

"Spades," Karen answered smiling, "I want to break your Celli into a New Ass Beating."

Karen was a slim, 18-year-old White girl who was in jail for killing her own baby. She is from a middle-class family that didn't want her to get pregnant, but she did anyway at 15-years-old. She hid the pregnancy for 9 months from her family. One day on her way to school she went to a Porta Potty and gave birth to the baby. She did the unthinkable and let the baby drown. She was willing to allow her baby to die in order to keep her pregnancy a dark secret. She was under 18 so, they gave her 6 years in prison. When she turns 21 she will be released. The "Baby Killer" is what they called her when she got to Silent Hill. She stayed in the juvenile facility 3 years before going to adult prison when she turned 18. As a matter of fact, she came in on her birthday. She would sit and cry all the time. She tried to kill herself twice. One of those times she tried to hang herself with some shoelaces on the stairwell which broke due to her weight. She fell and broke both her legs. Then she met Verna in the Infirmary and they became friends. Verna is like a big sister to her.

Fran said to Verna, "I'm not that good so if I mess up don't get mad."

"That's alright, we all mess up until we get the hang of it."

The four women sat playing cards; Verna, Fran, Karen, and Carla. They played until everyone had to lock in for count time and lights out.

LESSON 22

Knowledge is a Weapon You Should Always be Armed With

The next day came when Fran heard someone yell, "Chow time! You have 3 minutes to get ready!"

"Sometimes you don't have time to wash your face if you want to eat," Verna said as Fran got up still tired and sleepy.

"I'm okay, I don't want any. I'll wait until lunch to eat."

"Alright, see you in a few," Verna said as she closed the door.

The guard came to the cell a little bit after they called breakfast and told Fran she had a medical appointment after lunch. Then she fell back to sleep and drifted off into a dream where she found herself talking to Bill. She was telling him to pay the Warden off so he could recommend parole and she could get out. He told her she needed to be locked up because she is a Whore.

"Who are you calling a Whore!?" she screamed as she woke up back in prison.

"Fran, you alright?" as she opened her eyes Verna asked, "what did you have a bad dream?"

"I guess so," she answered.

The day went on, Fran went to lunch and ate and what they had wasn't that bad she said. And yes, Verna wanted Fran's leftovers.

"I'm going to start calling you Ms. Piggy," Fran said.

"Why is that?" Verna responded.

"Because you're a real Pig, you'll probably eat Shit if someone cooked it right."

"I don't think so."

"I can't tell the way you eat everything in sight."

It was time for Fran to see the nurse. The guard walked her up to the medical office.

"Hi, Mrs. Freeman; I'm Nurse Shelly and I would like to take your blood pressure."

She took her pressure and said, "You have a good reading. Are you allergic to anything?"

"Yes," Fran responded.

"What?"

"Assholes! My husband's one and seafood."

"Can you eat tuna fish?" the nurse asked.

"Yes, but shellfish is what I can't have."

"So, other than that you're in good shape?"

"Not exactly. I was diagnosed with Human Immunodeficiency Virus short for H.I.V."

"How long have you had this disease?"

"Three years."

"Are you taking any medications?"

"Yes," Fran said.

"What are you taking now?"

"AZT, my doctor was trying other medications."

"Do you get side effects?"

"Sometimes I feel weak, dizzy, or lite headed. Other times I don't feel like eating. And certain foods just make me throw up."

The nurse told Fran to continue to take her meds and she would be just fine. "And if you're not feeling well put a Sick Call Slip in and I'll see you.

The medication you're taking may cause you to experience severe depression, strange thoughts, and angry behavior. Some patients have thoughts of suicide and few have actually done it. But this may occur if you have a history of mental illness. If you think that you're having these psychiatric symptoms also put a slip in to see me and Mental Health. Alright Mrs. Freeman, if you don't have anything more that will be all. I will order your medications and you will able to start tomorrow. Bye now, take care." Fran walked back to her cell block.

Fran had been at Silent Hill for 6 months before she got her first visit. Bill came to see how she was doing. He had to be checked for weapons and drugs. Some of the women visitors brought them drugs and cash. If they managed to sneak by the guards; they could sell them and buy them too, if they got away with it. Sometimes they would kiss the visitor in the mouth to make the pass off. Another way would be to put it in their vagina or in their butt. Anyway, to get it in they would do it. Some inmates paid guards off to look the other way. And some paid with sexual favors.

Bill came in all dressed up like he just came from a meeting. He sat waiting patiently for Fran to come in. The guards finally brought her in and she sat down.

"Hey, what took you so long to come and see me?" she asked.

"I have been really tied up with work and couldn't get a day off. But I haven't forgot about you. Did you get the letter I sent you?"

"Yes, I did. I also got the money you sent me. One thousand dollars will be just fine for right now. If I need anything else, I'll let you know."

"So how are they treating you in here?" Bill asked.

"It's okay, but it's no walk in the park."

"I know you can take care of yourself," said Bill.

"I'm doing what I have to do. Some of these women are Crazy. It's one that is always throwing kisses at me. I try to ignore her, but she won't give up. I think I may have to poke out her Lecherous Eyes if she does not stop. Or I'll beat the Crap out of her; whichever comes first." Bill chuckles a little bit.

"What's so funny?" Fran asked him as her face distorted into an angry frown, "I may have to hurt this woman and you know what? If that guard was not over there I would slap your face."

"Why?" he said.

"Because you're laughing at me when I'm hurting."

"I'm so sorry Sweetheart," he said, "how are you feeling as far as the medications?"

"I feel sick sometimes, but other than that, I'm alright. How are you doing?" she asked, "and how come you didn't bring Tony with you?"

"I think he had a doctor's appointment."

"I want to know who she is and don't lie to me," Fran said looking into Bills eyes.

"Who's who?" he responds.

"The woman you're screwing."

"I'm not screwing anybody."

"Don't lie to me. I know if I'm not giving it to you, then you're getting it from somewhere. And when I was home, we never did it anyway."

"Aright! I met a lady, but we're just friends."

"Did you do her!?" she yelled.

"No! Our relationship fizzled after a month."

"Why was that?"

"Because I'm married to you."

"Bullshit!"

"Fran, I don't want to get into this. I didn't put you here; you put yourself here. So, don't make me out to be the bad guy. I remarried you because I love you. Besides that, you have 3 years to do."

"What do you mean 3 years to do? I have 5 years," she said.

"I have a friend on the parole board, you will do just three."

Then Fran smiled and said, "Do I now? Thank you, Sweetheart. Sorry for getting mad at you. Imma keep it real with you. I don't care who you screw while I'm in here. Just take care of my business; you are your own man. I have to live in here not out there with you. If I do that, this thing will kill me for sure."

"What thing?"

"My illness."

"Oh that," Bill said.

Then the guard yelled, "Visiting hours are now over!"

"I gotta go, so give me a hug."

"Sure, I love you."

"I love you too."

Bill waved at Fran as he walked out the door. Fran sat there waiting for the guard to take her back to her housing area. She felt a little jealous, but she knew jealousy could be a cruel taskmaster and she wanted no part of it. Fran thought about Tony and how he and Jennifer were doing with the baby. So, she decided to call. Then she dialed the number. The operator told her to say her name so, she did. And the person on the other line accepted her call.

"Thank you for using Diamond Phone Service."

"Hello. Who is this?"

"It's Jennifer," she answered.

"Hello Fran, how are you doing?"

"I'm doing just fine considering I can't go anywhere or do anything I like. But other than that, I'm alright."

"Where's Tony?" she asked.

"Hold on, I'll get him."

"Hello, Mom. How's it going in the Big House?"

"Not as bad as I thought it would be," she replied.

"Hey Mom, I got a joke for ya."

"What is it?"

"What kind bird can't fly?"

"I don't know. What kind?"

"A jailbird."

"Ha, ha, ha, that's real funny."

"Cheer up Mom, I just wanted to make you smile."

"That one didn't get it; try again. So, how's the baby?" she asked.

"Oh, he is just fine."

"And how is Renay's mother?"

"She alright too, I guess. I had to fire her from the job I gave her. She stopped coming to work after 3 paychecks. I'm gonna rehire her in a few weeks."

"That's good," Fran responded.

"Hey Mom I hate to cut you off, but I'm waiting on a very important phone call. Can you call back later?"

"Sure."

"Talk to you later then," he said.

"The nerve of that boy cutting me off like that. Well, that's how people treat you when you're locked up."

She felt a little down and was not going to call Tony back. She had an explosion of feelings that made her come to the realization that she may not make it home alive. And the poison in her blood may kill her. Then someone tapped Fran on the shoulder it was Verna.

"Heeeey. What's going on?"

"Oh, nothing, just thinking," Fran said.

"About What?" Verna asked.

"It's nothing."

"Fran if something is bothering you; you can talk to me about it."

"I'm alright!" she said in a firm voice.

"Okay then let's go to the yard and get some air," Verna suggested.

"How does it feel outside?"

"It's in the mid 70's."

"That's warm," Fran replied.

The guard then yelled, "You have two minutes to make your mind up, or you'll be locked in or locked out!"

The women got 2 hours in the Exercise Yard; that's where they made their drug deals, die from stab wounds and got beat downs. The guards in the tower can't see everything, but they sure try. They're up there armed with binoculars and high-powered rifles.

Fran and Verna walked around the yard a few times until someone waved at them telling them to come over. It was Joyce Lopez. She was in Cell Block B a Tier down from Fran's housing area.

"Who is that?" Fran asked Verna.

"That's Neno Perez's sister," she said as she continued to walk toward her.

"I will wait over here," Fran said suspiciously, "I may be a blonde, but I'm not stupid. You might be trying to set me up. I don't know you like that."

"Be cool. Fran, I would never do you like that. You're my friend. If it makes you feel any better. Wait here and I'll go and talk to her."

Fran gave Verna her critical eye and said, "Go head." Then Verna walked over to Joyce.

"What's up Girl?" Verna asked.

Then Joyce asked, "Who's your friend over there?"

"Her name is Fran."

"Is that the chick who killed my brother?" she asked.

"What are you going to do?" Verna asked.

"Nothing," Joyce answered, "I don't know what went on between those two. That was my brother and I can't bring him back. He treated women like Shit! So, I can't get into it. I go home next year and I'm not gonna let anything get in the way of that. Tell her to come over, I want to meet her. It's cool." Verna waved at Fran telling her to come over and join them. Then she walked toward the women.

"Hey, what's up?" she asked.

Then Joyce said, "How are you doing? You don't have to worry about me; that thing between you and my brother, I have nothing to do with it. I don't want to be your friend, nor your enemy but stay out my way."

"That's fine, nice meeting you," said Fran.

"Take care yourself because the walls have ears," Joyce said sarcastically. Fran and Verna walked away.

The women decided to walk around the yard a few more times and talk. This time Gina is walking behind them; her and two other women.

"Hey, Blondie."

"Who are you talking too?" Fran responded.

"You," Gina answered, "the one I want to get to know better."

"I don't want to get to know you. I want to you to leave me the Fuck alone you Lesbo Bitch before I beat the Black off you!" The Women started to fight and the guard told them to break it up.

Gina looked Fran up and down and said, "Your mine Bitch! Imma show you what we do to White Bitches like you, believe that!" As the smile on her face vanished.

"I don't know what to do Verna?"

"What about?"

"Gina. I don't think I should go to the guard because then they will call me a snitch. Then I'll really have problems. I should just beat her Ass and maybe she'll leave me alone. I don't want any trouble, but I have to do something." Fear lurked in every dark corner of her mind.

"Verna, what do I do?" Fran asked as she grabbed Verna's hand real tight.

"I don't know," Verna replied with a perplexed expression.

Fran looked at Verna and asked, "Do you want something to eat?"

"Yes. What do you have?"

"Damn you greedy; I was just playing with you to see what you would say. And you say just what I thought you would say. Nothing. Do you have anything between your ears?"

"Yes, I do. It's called a brain."

"Is it on?" Fran asked, "never mind. Let's go play cards or something. Talking to you is like talking to a wall, I get nothing back."

"I'm sorry I can't help you, Fran, I'm new at this. I got problems too."

"I'm sorry too for saying those mean things to you," said Fran.

"It's okay. You're under a lot of stress."

"You got that right Sister," Fran said as she put her head down.

Fran did find that predators like to size you up before they make their move. Like a jackal finding that their prey is as weak as it looks.

As time when on, she got a job to keep her from staying on the tier all day. She started working in the Laundry Room, and Gina worked there too. Fran was upset to see that she was also employed there.

"I'm gonna kill this Snake Bitch and then they are going to give me life," Fran thought to herself as she folded the clothes.

Verna got a job in the kitchen, she must be near food. She told Fran, food makes her feel good, it's like sex, she gotta have it. And that's why she gained so much weight.

After Fran went to the canteen a few times she brought Verna her own snacks and she ate hers up and then wanted what Fran had brought for herself. Sometimes she would give it to her and sometimes she would tell Verna to get out of her face.

LESSON 23

Happy is the Man or Woman that Finds Wisdom
And Man, or Woman that Gets Understanding

Fran started liking her job in the Laundry Room. It killed a lot of time and it also gave her a chance to clear her of thoughts of everyday prison life. She did not feel she belonged there with those other women. She knew she was not innocent of her crime, but felt it was justified. But she had taken someone's life. When she crossed that line, there was no coming back. And her society connections would not save her from the wolves who lie and wait for her blood.

Fran also found it confronting to think of her mother; who she missed very much. At that moment, she was swept away by a flood of tears as waves of emotions that ignited the hate within her. Because her father took her mother from her and she wished on that dark day in her life that father would have been suddenly stricken with reason. And maybe her mother would still be alive. She loved her mother and felt he cheated her out of her vengeance by committing suicide those many years ago, that left her in anguish.

"I would have rather killed my father instead of Neno," she thought herself, "and maybe I would not be here. I would have gotten away with murder with all the pain he caused me and my mother would still be here."

Then someone was tapping Fran on the shoulder, "Hey you! Get up and take that cart of clothes to the Supply Room!"

It was the guard that works the 8 to 4 shift Ms. Downs. She was a tall Black lady with short hair, 30-years-old, kind of chubby with a cute face.

"If you want to keep your job, I suggest you stay awake. And I know you don't need the money, but it's better than sitting on the tier doing nothing."

"I guess you're right," Fran said.

"I want to ask you something," Ms. Downs said.

"What?" Fran answered.

"I want to know if you need anything?"

"Like what?"

"Things you might want from outside."

"I don't know. Let me think about it and I'll let you know," Fran said, "but I know It's gonna cost me, right?"

"It might cost you a little, it might cost you a lot; but it is gonna cost you," the woman said.

"I want to know how do I pay you? Do I pay you in canteen snacks? Or do I write you a check? If we come to an agreement I will pay you $50 every time you bring me something in; most of the time it will be food."

"That's fine."

"When you write your pay to, make the check out to Foxtail Real Estate Company."

"Write down all of your information for me," Fran told the smiling guard.

She knew she just hit a gold mine because she knew everybody needed something. Especially people who have money to spend. And Fran had more than she could spend in a lifetime. And she would protect her investment and hopes Fran would need her all the time. Because she had 3 kids and a prison paycheck was not enough to feed them, herself, and pay rent. She not only wanted to be Fran's mule, but her friend also. She knew she was rich and had money.

"I want you to keep our little conversation between us."

"Alright," Fran agreed, "I would not want to mess up a good thing."

"Neither do I," the guard said, "I still need you to work."

"Alright." Then Fran pushed the cart to the supply room.

"I saw you staring at me from the corner of my eye," Fran said to Gina.

"I was just walking by and I couldn't help but see you talking to the police.

"What you snitching now?" Gina asked.

"No, I'm not."

"I can't tell you were over there for 10 minutes taking about something, you must've been talking about you and me," said Gina.

"What the Fuck is your problem Gina?"

"I want to feel your Nice Petite Ass. I want to feel your lips on mine."

"Keep dreaming Freak," Fran said as she walked away from her.

"You're still mine Bitch."

"Fuck you!"

"I intend you," Gina said with a smile.

Ms. Downs walked by and asked, "What's going on between you two?"

"Nothing," Fran said, "I was telling her I would see her on the tier." Fran lied because she didn't want to be seen as a snitch. The women would hate her if they thought she was telling anything.

"Stay away from her, she's a little off her rocker," Ms. Downs told Fran.

"I sure will."

"Good."

"I'm going to take all of you back to your blocks now." And the women lined up to go back; Gina, Fran, Carla, Ramona, and Mardovia.

The women were tired and wanted to go back, relax, watch TV and eat. *Fran thought about what Ms. Downs said about bringing stuff into the prison that she needs. But what she really wanted was a large cheese steak with everything on it with a Grape soda and she would have to share with Verna.*

"I have a guard in my pocket," she thought to herself, "an alliance with a Correctional Officer was a pleasant change that would make her stay more comforting. But the thought of paying $50 for a cheesesteak was insane, but she is risking her job to help Fran, so the money is nothing. She'll be eating food from the streets and not that State slop that she would get used to eating one way or another.

Fran reached her tier and went to her cell. There was something on the window; a towel. So, Fran thought Verna must be taking a crap or something. But then she heard lite moaning from the cell. So, she knocked on the door out of concern for Verna, thinking she might be sick so, she called her.

A voice came from the cell, "Hold up!"

But Fran noticed some of the towels had fallen from her knocking on the door. So, she looks in the small opening of the window and seen Verna with her legs spread eagle letting some unknown women performing oral sex on her.

Fran was shocked for a minute. But she knew Verna was that way so, it was expected. And then she heard more moaning, but this time more intense.

The voice from the cell said, "Fran I'm coming, give me a minute!"

"I bet you are you Little Freak."

So, the guard called count time. Fran knocked on the door again. The door opened. Verna stepped out first to see if the coast was clear, with the cells open it was a good time to move. The woman emerged unleashed from her sexual frustrations and did not even look Fran's way. She wanted to get away as fast as she could. She felt embarrassed and walked away with her head down.

Fran walked into the cell and said to Verna, "In here getting your Freak on I see."

"It wasn't like that."

"So, if it wasn't like that…why was the towel up on the window?" she asked.

"We were just talking."

"Talking about what?"

"You don't have to lie to me. Besides, I saw you through the little hole in the window. And I don't care what you do, just take care of yourself. I wish someone would have told me what I'm telling you right now. I know from experience that lust dims thoughts of consequences. And do you know this person to let her have her way with you? And do you know where she's been? Think about your life and what it means to you. Don't become a slave to sex, because if you're not careful, it will destroy you, and you'll become like I am," Fran said.

"How are you?" Verna asked while looking at Fran's eyes trying to read her soul because she's about to reveal a profound truth and a hard lesson of life.

"I'm here because of my own doing. I use to pay for sex from certain guys. And one of these men gave me HIV and it changed my life forever. I did not kill him because he gave me HIV. I killed him because he did not use a condom. It was my own fault; I should have protected me."

Then Verna asked Fran, "How long have you had the disease?"

"Three years," she answered, "just use protection. If you let someone taste your goods use a dental dam, Saran wrap or cut a condom. Or don't have sex at all. Using one condom beats taking a whole lot of medication, trust me. See right now you're young, stupid, wet behind your ears, and looking for love in all the wrong places. Don't let these women turn you out; you're still young. Be somebody when you get out of here. I will even help you out, just show me you want something out of life."

Verna is now smiling and tells Fran, "I will never disrespect the cell again."

"I mean it's your cell too; just be careful. I want to see you make it. Don't make the same mistakes I did. Don't let a few moments of pleasure change who you are. Learning to accept the truth is the first step to gaining control of your destiny. Use care, use your head and you'll have the best chance for success. I wish I had learned early on about life and what to expect. And don't let anyone discourage you from your goals and dreams. Because if you do, 'Dreams' they will 'Remain' and they will 'Never' grow to become what you pictured in your mind and in your heart."

"Thank you, Fran, I needed that; it shows me that you care about me. I know I haven't known you long, but God must have sent you to me just to tell me what you told me. I will no longer allow myself to be used as a doormat by those vultures who want to pick my bones clean or lick them clean or whatever comes first."

Then Fran said, "I'm going to say one more thing and then I'm going to lay down. A messenger is often blamed for the message."

"What does that mean?" Verna asked.

"A many of people have been killed for their message. So, don't blame me when your problems don't get better. Stay strong and keep your behavior in check. And your success lies over the horizon," Fran said and then turned over and went to sleep.

Verna woke Fran up and asked if she could have one of her cakes. All that talking made her hungry.

"Yes Verna, and please remind me to never talk to you when I got food around, Ms. Piggy." And Fran went back to sleep.

The next day Fran and Verna went to the prison chapel to enjoy the church service for a few hours. That's where they would meet other inmates from other cell blocks. They also passed off love letters to one another. And some of the females would go to the restroom to do their business. If the guard became suspicious, he would clear them out and make go back to their seats.

Fran and Verna set in the first row away from those gossiping women in the back. The congregation began to sing Amazing Grace. Fran stood to her feet, as did the entire church. And they began to praise God through song. Fran thanked God for His protection, for her family and that He forgave her for her sins. The chaplain thanked everyone for coming and then started to preach.

"Turn your Bibles to Deuteronomy 8; that part of the Bible tells how Moses lead the people of God through the desert for 40 years because they had sinned against Him. But he wanted them to remember what God had done for them all those years. And Moses said to the people of God, "Make sure you follow every command that I'm giving you today. Then you will live, you will increase in your numbers; then you will enter the land and take it as your own. It's the land the Lord promised with an oath to your people long ago. Remember, how the Lord your God lead you all the way. He guided you in the desert for these 40 years." And it went on to say, "The Lord your God is bringing you into a good land. It has streams and pools of water. Springs flow in its valleys and hills. It has wheat, barley, vines, fig trees, pomegranates, olive oil, and honey. There is plenty of food in that land. You will have everything that you need. When you have eaten, and have been satisfied; praise the Lord your God. Praise Him for the land He has given you. But supposed to don't obey His commands?"

The preacher went on to say, "Suppose you have plenty to eat, you build fine houses and settle down in them. Your herds and flocks increase in their numbers; you also get more and more silver and gold. And everything you have will multiply. Then your heart will become proud. And you will forget the Lord your God," he said.

He continued to say, "This applies to you today. It also says this is verse 18. But remember the Lord your God, He gives you the ability to produce wealth. Don't forget the Lord your God, and don't worship any other Gods, don't follow or bow down to them. I give witness against you today, that if you do, you will certainly be destroyed. You will be destroyed just like the nations the Lord your God is destroying to make room for you. That's what will happen if you don't obey Him."

The preacher spoke on the goodness of Jesus, the women prayed and some gave their heart to the Lord. Fran said the preacher was talking about her because God did increase everything she had and fed her when she did not have anything to eat. And she knew God was with her even though she has HIV. He will tenderly protect her from dire circumstance. Verna felt God's love also as tears ran down her face as she asked God to make her a better person. And what she asked of God, He had already done. He spoke to Verna's heart through Fran's words that day she caught her with another woman.

The service ended and all of them started returning to their cell blocks; feeling heightened and free from worry. Then a fight broke out between two women who were fighting over another woman. One of the females said the other women had asked her girlfriend for sex. They kicked, scratched, and pulled each other hair. Clothes were ripped. One of the girls' breast were hanging out. The guards finally came to the girl's rescue as she bled from her nose. Also, one of her eyes were half closed. But before the fight was stopped, she caught a kick to the face by a spectator who started the whole thing. The two women were handcuffed. The one that was beaten severely was taken to an outside hospital for a broken nose and a collapsed lung from being kicked in the side. The two women were charged with assault and was to be put in maximum security for 15 days. They would be allowed out once a day for exercise. Once they are taken to court, they could get additional time.

Some people come to prison with less than a few months, but end up never leaving because they do something stupid and get life. Therefore, you can't let people push you around in a place like this. If one does it, everyone else will think they can try you also and take advantage of you. And you may have to defend yourself and who knows the outcome. Prison life is hard as Fran will soon find out.

Time went on and Fran became aware of her surroundings. She did not get mixed up in the gangs in the Stone Motel, but it proved to be a vital mistake. Most of the women were down with a clique, who protected them from other cliques. They would extort money, sex, drugs, cigarettes and food from women who wanted to remain neutral. But they had to pay a price for their neutrality with their blood or their possessions.

Gina was in a gang called, *"The Majestic Queens"* who were mostly women who liked other women; lesbians gone wild. A man would lose his mind to see the debauchery (excessive indulgence in sensual pleasures) that goes on behind these walls. The other gangs were *"The Lady Killers"* and *"The Jagged Edges"* who were Mexican and Spanish; nobody messes with those Bitches. If you fart around these chicks, they would cut your throat because of disrespect. They started a riot because one of The Lady Killers sneezed on the member of The Jagged Edges dinner by accident. Raina, a member of The Lady Killers, swore that was the case. But Asia of the Jagged Edges would not hear of it, and picked up her tray full of food with peas, mash potatoes, and gravy and smashed Raina in the face which stunned her for a moment. And at that second, pandemonium broke out; women from both gangs were throwing trays, food, and chairs. Guards with riot gear had to be called in because the prison had a low tolerance for that type of behavior. The prison would blame only one person because they couldn't put everyone in Maximum Security. The "Hole" is what they call it. Even though Asia started the fight, she and Raina both would be sent to the "Hole" and the prison would be put on lockdown for a few days. They will eat in their cells, have no visits, no commissary, and they will have ham and cheese for dinner with one milk. And mail service is suspended also.

LESSON 24

Commemorate Your Love Forever in Your Memory
For Love Has No Boundaries

Bill Freeman is sitting with his back towards the window as he eats his dinner in a fine restaurant with his lady friend Clarissa Reno. She has never been married but wants to be if he is rich, can appreciate her taste for fine jewelry and has sex once a week. She would rather go shopping for precious metals than to have sex.

Clarissa met Bill at a dinner party; he looked at her and she reminded him of Fran when she was younger. He was standing at the bar having a drink; all the drinks were free.

But Clarissa walked up to Bill and said, "If these drinks were not free, I would have bought you one. And after that, I would introduce myself to you and you would do the same."

"Is that right? Well, you're definitely to die for," and then he kissed her hand and said, "I love your name Clarissa, its fits you, your name is as beautiful as you are and I must say you look dazzling in that dress."

"Thank you," she said, "you're not so bad yourself." And that's how Bill met Clarissa.

So, Clarissa and Bill are enjoying a quiet dinner and she asked him how his was wife doing?

"She's fine," he answered.

"Did you tell her about us and that we are going to get married as soon as she signs the divorce papers?"

"No, I did not," he replied.

"Why?"

"Because I will do it when the time is right; but I did tell her I met someone."

"Tell her before my birthday."

"Why is that?" he asked.

"Because I want to get married on that date."

"When is your birthday?"

"Three months from now. So, I expect you to tell her before then. Alright, Baby?"

"I will," he said sadly.

"How do you think she will take it?"

"I hope she takes it well. The first time she divorced me; now I'm going to divorce her."

Clarissa looked Bill right in the eye and said, "Do we have to give her anything like alimony?"

"We don't have to do anything! I'll handle that. Don't go worrying your pretty little self about that. It's none of your business."

"If I'm gonna be your wife, it is my business."

"Well, you're not my wife yet; I'll handle my business and you will handle yours. Alright?"

"Yes," Clarissa said with a disapproving look on her face.

"Don't worry about it, I love you now. I still love Fran though. She is the mother of my son and that is as far as it goes."

Bill took her hand and pulled her into a gentle kiss. She closed her eyes waiting for his lips to tenderly touch against hers as he heated her passion.

"That was nice," she said, "is there more where that came from?"

"Unlimited for you," as he kissed her again, "let's eat before we find ourselves under the table." She was then fanning herself with both hands.

"Did someone turn the heat up?" she asked.

"No, you're just hot for me," Bill replied. The two ate their dinner and finished with a night cap.

Bill drove her home to her condominium, which was not far away. Bill escorted Clarissa to her door and said, "You are a treasure who is so beautiful with features that would fire men's minds with memories of you."

"Do you think so?" Clarissa asked him pointing at her lips suggesting to Bill that he kiss her again. And he did.

"How's that?" he asked.

"Is that the more you were talking about?" she asked with a big smile.

"You know it is," he whispered, "but I have to go to work in the morning."

"I thought you might want seconds on dessert," Clarissa said.

"As good as that sounds I have to decline," he said walking away waving and blew her a kiss getting on the elevator.

On the way, down Bill was thinking about how he was going to tell Fran he was in love with another woman. Bill loved Fran, but he knew she had HIV and he did not love her that much to risk contracting her disease. He even thought of using condoms, but he quickly dismissed that idea because he could not bring himself to have sex with someone he knew was infected.

The first-time Fran told Bill that she was HIV positive he knew sex with her was gone forever. He did not want to tell her because she was already going through something menacing and he didn't want to add to the load she's carrying. Which is her parents are gone, she has been sexually assaulted as a young girl and she may die from this illness.

When Bill thought about this at that moment he felt a deep sadness in his heart, so much so that he pulled his car over on the side of the road and wept. It pained him to think about what she must be going through. He then thought about Clarissa and how lovely she looked tonight. And a lingering fragrance still filled the car of her essence as he inhaled her aroma.

"I will wait to tell her," he thought to himself. Although Fran did tell him she did not care what he does as long as he takes care of her business and her financial matters.

A few years before Fran was sent to prison, her and her business partner Linda Cates started a finance company with 2 million dollars. Fran put in a large portion of the money needed to get it started. She wanted Bill to make sure the business was going alright.

Bill gave Fran a 10 million settlement in their divorce. But Bill has a net worth over 100 million so that so a given and he quickly accepted her demand. But he remarried her because he felt sorry for her and she needed him to help her to be strong. But after Fran went to prison, he felt lonely and needed some companionship. And sometimes he would patronize call girls' services at $200 an hour. But after sex with these women he felt empty and disappointed. The sex may have been good with these Volumptuous females, but he wanted "Real Love" and he would not find it in a prostitute. That's where Clarissa came in, he wanted to feel alive again. He did not want to make the same mistakes he made with Fran when he married her all those years ago. Bill got to know her and he really liked her. This woman wants the finer things in life and Bill would give it to her if she played by his rules. He was getting older and wanted to live his life to the fullest; he just needed someone to live it with.

"Bill did not know if Fran would take him to the cleaners after he asked for a divorce, but she has her own money and a business to run once she gets out," he thought to himself, "or she may want some of his money because he has it and they are married."

Verna and Fran are sitting in their cell playing cards. The prison is still on lock down because of the fight in the dining area.

Fran said, "Verna this Shit is Crazy being locked up 3 days in here with you Farting every 5 minutes."

"I can't help it, that cheese popcorn gives me gas."

"Tell me about it," Fran said holding her nose.

"I think I got to…"

"I think I got to what?" Fran asked.

"I got to take a Shit," Verna replied, "and yes, you have to smell it."

"Don't remind me, can't you hold it until they let us out?"

"Nope, I got go right now!" Verna said and then she pulled her pants down and sat on the toilet.

"I'm going to cover my head," said Fran, "you stink."

"Thank you for telling me; now I know how to get on your nerves, just take a dump when we're on lock down," said Verna.

"And I'm gonna beat the White off your Ass; try that again and I'll make you Shit in your pants! And then it will really STINK!" Fran said pissed.

Verna said, "Oh, looks like I can't win. Yelp! Gotta go! Gotta go!"

"Somebody save me!" Fran said playfully.

The next day everything returned to normal; the women went to breakfast and then to work. Verna went to work at 4 in the morning; she worked during breakfast and lunch. She would get off at 2pm. Fran's hours were 8am to 4pm; sometimes Verna would bring food back to the cell and have a party; just two friends enjoying each other's company. Ms. Downs Greeted Fran when she got to work.

"Hey Fran, did you think about what you wanted me to bring you?"

"Yes, I sure did," Fran said.

"What?"

"I want a large cheese steak with everything on it."

"Is that all?" the guard asked.

"Yes," she answered, "I'll send the check to the address you gave once I get the goods."

"Sounds like a winner," the guard said, "now we got work to do." Then she pointed at the stack of clothes that needed to be sorted and folded.

"I will bring your steak in tomorrow and you don't have to go to the chow hall, you can eat it in the break room," the guard said to Fran.

"Can I save some for later?" Fran asked.

"No, I rather you ate it here. That way, nobody knows anything because someone might see you eating it and get jealous. And they tell someone, who would tell somebody else snitching, and there goes my job. And then I'll be looking for you to give me one."

"I'll tell you what, if all goes well or if it doesn't I'll give you one. Or I'll get someone to hire you with better pay," said Fran.

"And you would do that for me?" the guard asked smiling at her, "and the would be very nice, thank you, Fran. I won't let you down."

"You just get that sandwich to me."

"Sure thing, Boss."

"Don't call me that, someone may be ease dropping and I won't get my pizza, I mean cheese steak."

"You want a slice of pizza too?" the guard asked.

"No, just the steak. I don't want to overwhelm you with a lot of stuff. We will work on the pizza in a few days."

"Okay, Boss."

"Stop that!" Fran yelled but in a soft voice.

"I work for you now so, if I get fired so what."

"Don't get careless, I need you around if I'm here," Fran immediately said as she walked into the infamous laundry supply closet.

If the walls could talk, the laundry supply closet would tell a many of stories. And many more would find their place among the dingy dirty clothes, behind the huge dryers, and between the washers.

There is one story that stood out more than any other, it was when a guard named Tommy Warbucks and a female inmate named Janet Fox were locked in the laundry closet together. Tommy had been working for about 5 years at the prison and he had a problem with keeping his hands off the inmates. He loved his job, it was like letting the fox watch the hen house. The guard would promise to bring in food and drugs, but would never deliver on his promises. He would get the new inmates and trick them into giving him sexual favors.

Janet was a nice girl who was only going to be there for 90 days. Tommy told her he would put $100 in her account, but she did not tell him that she was an epileptic and could have a seizure at any moment. So, Janet agreed to give the guard a Blow Job.

And before she commenced to unbuckling his pants she said, "I want my money!"

"You'll get it," he said.

"I better." And she began to pleasure him.

He began to moan. "Yes, that's it, get it all," he said. Janet's body began to jerk.

Tommy said, "What's up with you?" And at that moment, his pleasure turned to pure pain as Janet's jaws locked down on his Penis; he screamed at the top of his lungs.

Then she went into convulsions as he beat her on the head yelling, "Let it Go! Let it Go!"

Someone heard the guard screaming, but the door was locked and no one could get in because he had the key. They had to use a crowbar to pry the door open. When they got the door open, Janet was still shaking with Tommy's Penis still in her mouth with Tommy detached from it. And he was going into shock. They started to relax Janet and she relaxed her jaws. And the Paramedics were called to retrieve Tommy's Penis from the women clamped shut mouth.

When the Paramedics arrived, Tommy yelled, "The Bitch bit my 'DICK OFF! Can they put it back on!?" he cried.

"Calm down," the medic said, "I'll give you something for pain."

"Calm down!? You Calm down…your Dick's not on ICE, Mine IS! You Here Me!?"

The man was taken to the hospital and the doctors sewed his Penis back on. The Warden told Tommy Warbucks as long as he stayed in the hospital, he had a job. The moment he stepped out of it, he was fired.

The women sued the state saying that Tommy Warbucks forced her to have sex with him even though it was a mutual agreement. Janet will get more than the $100 that was owed to her. The state gave Janet a settlement of 10,000. She claimed emotional distress and said she was in fear of her life. Also, she did not know what he wanted her to do to him and that's what triggered her seizure. In addition, Mr. Warbucks lost his Penis and the doctors were able to save it. Janet was then released 20 days later. A nice payday for doing something she likes. I don't think she meant to bite his Pecker off, but she knew it could happen.

MEN SHOULD BE WARNED!

IF A WOMAN IS EPILEPTIC DO NOT GO PUTTING YOUR "DICK" IN HER MOUTH BECAUSE YOU MAY LOSE IT!!!

LESSON 25

If You've Learned from the Past and Received Good Instructions Don't Hesitate to Move Forward

As time went on, Fran and Ms. Downs became good friends and she supplied all her needs. Ms. Downs made good money working for Fran, she even had her doing work on the streets delivering messages to certain people when she could not get them on the phone. Ms. Downs also became her bodyguard when she worked. The Warden even wanted in on the action.

He called Fran to his office, "Hello Mrs. Freeman, how are you doing out there in the land of the lost?"

"I'm doing alright," she said.

"The reason I called you is to see if you need anything, wanted to talk or just need a friend. I also wanted to know if you need me to talk to someone regarding parole, early release or any concerns you may have. I'm at your service."

"That's good to know Warden," Fran said, "are you asking to help me or do you want me to ask you to help me?"

"I just want to help out where I can," he said.

"For a price, I assume?"

"I must say, you may be right in your assumption," Mr. Swells said.

"And what will you price be and for what service will you be providing?" Fran asked.

"I want to start by saying," As he picked up some papers on his desk and he read a few lines off it, "I see you're serving a 5-year sentence, but if you read the paper in front of you; you will see the amount that I require which is $15.000. I will guarantee I will have you home in a year. You've been with us for about 9 months. Therefore, I may be able to pull some strings and it may be sooner." Fran looked at the Warden so happy she could not speak.

She said, "When do you need the money?"

"As soon as you can get it," he said smiling.

"I'll call some people and have the check sent to your home."

"Very well. I look forward to working with you Mrs. Freeman."

"Likewise," she said as she got up to leave.

He looked her in her eyes and said, "Everything is not for everyone. If you know what I mean."

"Gotcha," she said and then walked out feeling like a new woman because soon she will be able to go home. Her money was her power and she felt optimistic that everything would work out.

"I have Kimberly Downs working for me and now the Warden," she thought to herself.

Fran came to prison alone and scared, but those feelings were deteriorating fast. Then she quickly realized that everyone around her was looking for a payout and would jeopardize their jobs and careers to get their hands on her money. But as long as she got what she wanted, they could have it.

The guard that works 8 to 4 told Fran if she wanted another job, she could have it. Anyone she wanted too. But she chooses to stay in the Laundry Room with Ms. Downs, her bodyguard with a badge. And Gina and her crew would not scare her off that easy, she was staying right there. Disregarding that Gina wanted her in some way. So, she had to keep her eyes opens and her ears tuned into what might be coming down the pike. Fran could not understand why Gina wanted to mess with her being almost 40-years-old. Old enough to be her mother, twice around or her grandmother.

Tony came to see Fran one day; him, Little Mark and Jennifer. They all came in the Visitors Room and sat down.

"Hey mom, how are you doing?" Tony asked.

"Just fine, it took you long enough to come see me," Fran said.

"I've been busy working and did not have the time to get away. I'm here now, that's all that matters," he said with a frustrated look on his face.

"I know there is something different about you," she said.

"There's nothing wrong with me," he said looking away from Fran.

She looked him right in the eyes and said, "You're smoking that SHIT again!"

"No, I'm not." Fran immediately turned and started talking to Jennifer and the baby.

"How are you doing Ms. Lady and what have you been doing with yourself? Hope you're now smoking that Shit with this Dope Head."

"I'm not smoking anything." Then she cut her off too and started talking directly to the baby.

"How is my handsome Little Man doing?" Then he smiled.

Then she looked at Tony. "I see it in your face and you're losing weight," she said to him.

"I don't know what to tell you."

"I think you got this Girl hooked on that Shit with you. Didn't you?"

"No, I did not!" he responded angrily.

"Still in denial I see," Fran said with a mischievous look on her face.

"I don't have to sit here and listen to you!" Tony yelled.

Fran responded real calmly, "You should listen to somebody."

Tony stood up and said, "I'm leaving!"

"Bye, I'm surprised you're not gone by now," Fran said as she looked at Jennifer, "leave that STUFF alone and then leave him alone."

"But I love him."

"You love toilet paper too. But after you wipe your Ass you don't put it in your pocket."

Tony yelled to Jennifer, "Bring the baby and come on!"

"I think you should go," she said to Jennifer.

"I love you, Tony," Fran said as she waved, "I just don't want you to make the same mistakes you made 7 years ago, Jen remember, toilet paper is alright to have around when you are not wiping your Ass with it. But once it has Shit on it; flush it."

Jennifer looked at Fran and said, "I'll see you soon." And they left.

Tony was very angry that his mother talked to him that way. But she was right, he did start Jennifer getting high. She was becoming a Pain in the Ass. She smoked more Cocaine than he did. He created a monster. She was bigger than he was. He was a dope fiend with money and he will be broke in two years. But in reality, he would always have money because his father has it and would help him out at any time, as he did some time ago.

Fran felt alright telling her son to get his life together. Then she went back to work. Her visit was only 15 minutes; she had 30 minutes left because visits are 45 minutes. And when she got back to work, Ms. Downs wondered why she was back so soon so she asked her.

"Why are you back from your visit so soon?"

"I pissed my son off by telling him the truth about himself. I think he's back using drugs."

"What do you mean, he's back?"

"Just like I said. An old girlfriend of his mother got him into drugs. At least, that is what he told me." Fran worked the rest of her shift and returned to her cell block to call Bill and ask him about Tony's drug use.

Fran reached Bill, "Hello Mr. Freeman."

"Hey Fran, how are you doing?"

"I'm fine, but I can't say the same for Tony. He looks like Shit. Have you seen him?"

"Yes, I have. He looks fine to me," Bill said.

"I think he's back on that Shit."

"What Shit?" he asked.

"Drugs Stupid!"

"Oh, that? I knew when I called him and he was always in the shower. I knew then. But I haven't spoken to him concerning that. I want to speak to you about something else."

"What?" she said.

"I have been thinking that we should separate, get a divorce."

"We just got married," she said.

"I know. But I'm in love with someone else. It's not like I don't love you, I don't think it will work between us."

"Is it because I have HIV?" she asked.

"No," he answered.

"Yes, it is!" she said angrily.

"I still love you, but I do not want to be with you."

"Is that right," she said, "I can live with that. The spark is gone. There is nothing left, but our son."

"Let's be friends," Bill said.

"Sure, we can be friends after you give me 2 million dollars."

"I can do that," he said. *Thinking to himself, "Is that all?" Smiling on the other end of the phone.*

"I will have my lawyer send you the documents to sign and then we will work out the terms of the divorce later on," Bill said.

"I surprised you didn't I when I said all I wanted was a measly 2 million dollars. I could take you for more than that. And of course, if you fight, you would lose. But I don't want to fight anymore. I made you pay me 10 million in the first divorce so right now I'm just fine. And when I receive the documents, I will sign them when I'm good and ready."

"Just sign them at your convenience."

"I intend to," she said frowning.

"I have to go," Bill said, "I'll talk to you later."

"Okay, Bye." And Fran hangs the phone up feeling more hurt than she was showing.

"I don't need him," she thought to herself. Because she has friends who want to see her home and she has money.

Fran wanted to cry, but the tears would not come because the heart doesn't lie. She never loved Bill the way he loved her. But as time went on, she learned to love him a little, but never whole heartily. Because if she truly loved him the way he loved her; he'd would have known by the way she spoke his name and the way she kissed him. And if their lovemaking were passionate and she tenderly spoke to his heart. Also, by her actions, he would never leave her no matter what the circumstance. Because true love is like a candle. It will melt down but never melts away.

Fran was good at concealing things from people, but she could not hide it from herself. She was hurt, but if there was no one special in his life; she was alright with that. He could do whatever he wanted, except, have another woman. It was like she didn't want him, but she didn't want anyone else to have him either. She was selfish and only cared about herself. A feeling of immense jealousy overtook her emotions.

"I won't sign those papers at all. Maybe I won't give him a divorce after all and contest it.

Fran was so upset she went into her cell and laid down. Verna was watching the TV and Fran told her to turn that Shit off.

"But I'm watching this show."

"I don't care!" she yelled. Then Verna turned off the TV.

"What's eating you?"

"Nothing," Fran said.

"I'm going to play cards until you cool off," Verna said.

"Bye! And close the door behind you!" Then Verna slammed the door real hard.

Scared the Living Shit out of Fran who yelled, "You Fat Ass Toad!" She laid there for a few minutes and then went to the door and called Verna. She came back.

"What do you want?" she asked, "did you get the little man out of your Ass?"

"Look, Verna, I'm sorry for acting Crazy. Do you want to finish watching the TV? You can."

"I'm cool, I'm playing cards now. And I accept your apology."

"Give me hug Girl," Fran said with her arms wide open, "I'm sorry again."

"Don't be sorry be careful," Verna said smiling.

"And don't be using my words on me," Fran quickly responded.

"I'll see you later. I'm going to finish kicking some Ass in Spades." Verna returned to the card table.

The women at the table were talking about a woman named Marsha Dennis who was having a relationship with the guard for about 3 months. The entire time she was having sex with him she was saving the semen either in a condom or after a Blow Job; she would spit it in a cup, let it dry out and then put it in an envelope. She is serving 20 years for a bank robbery and now she's suing the state for money and freedom just like Janet did. The women are normally gossiping about who was getting out, who was messing with who, who got cut, who committed suicide, and who came to see who. And women at the table asked Verna what's up with her cellmate.

"Who Fran?" she responded, "she's alright."

"No, she's not," the woman said, "she's always talking to the guard. I hope she's not telling."

"She's not telling," Verna said, "she's not even like that."

"I hope not," the women said.

"You Bitches leave her alone, that's my friend. She's good people. She just wants to do her time and go home!"

"Tell her to watch her back or stay away from the guard. Because we think she's telling."

The guard on the tier yelled, "Count Time!" and the girls went in their cells for the night.

The next day, Fran called her lawyer and told him what Jake Swells told her about going home within a year; and for him to send a check for $15,000 to the Warden's home. And also, make sure her investments are paying off and about her impending divorce. And that she wants Bill to give her 2 million dollars so, that she can donate it to fight HIV and AIDS. And he will hate that.

"He will," the lawyer repeated, "but it's yours. You can do with it as you want. I will have a talk with Mr. Swells."

"Alright," Fran said, "call you soon. Bye."

Fran has been taking her HIV medicine for 9 months and some days she does not feel well. Therefore, she wants to stay in bed all day and Verna helps take care of her too. Fran takes 3 medications as a complete regimen. She is not having that many side effects with her new medications. However, she has trouble sleeping, concentrating, has crazy dreams and must deal with constant diarrhea. Fran's medications help block HIV-1 reverse transcriptase, a viral chemical in the body (an enzyme) that is needed for HIV-1 to multiply. It also helps increase the number of T-Cells. And CD4 T-Cells allowing her immune system to improve lowering the amount of HIV-1 in the blood. Which lowers the chance of death or infections that happen when the immune system is weak. Opportunistic infections will develop. She also risks getting Pneumonia and Herpes Virus Infections. And a condition called "Mycobacterium" avium complex short for MAC. But Fran is keeping her head up and won't let it get her down.

The guard gave out mail and Fran got a big tan envelope with her divorce documents from Bill. She was over the fact that he wanted another woman in his life. But she would not go quietly

"I will not give into whoever she is, I'm not giving into this disease or this Asshole who kicked me to the curb like garbage!"

Verna was Fran's new friend, but she was not without her prejudice ways and ill feelings towards her sickness. She would not eat after her. If she was eating something and could not finish it and offered it to Verna. She would act like she wanted it and flush it down the toilet when Fran turned her back. Whenever she finished using the toilet she would spray a it down with disinfecting cleaner like she has the plague or something.

Then one day she played a trick on Verna. She knew she was acting funny towards her. Fran opens a cake that she knows that Verna loves and took a bite and said, "I don't want this."

"I do," Verna said.

"No, you don't with Your Fake Ass."

LESSON 26

The Teacher Is In

If You're Willing to See Yourself in a Different Light;

A Glorious New Self Image Emerges When You Do

Fran told Verna to stop acting like she's going to catch HIV from the toilet seat.

"Verna let tell you something about HIV so, you can stop running around here all paranoid like if you touch something I've touched you'll catch it."

"I don't act like that."

"You do," Fran said, "you're the same person that would let a stranger eat your SNATCH, but you're scared to use the same bowl that I use. I think you would catch it from her before me. And the only way to get is from unprotected sex, a blood transfusion, through breast milk of an infected person, body fluids, and sharing needles. Look, Verna, I would not wish this on my worst enemy. I would never want you to go through this turmoil."

"I'm sorry," Verna said.

"I will understand if you want to get moved to another cell. I'll speak to Ms. Downs and see what I can do," said Fran.

"If you do I'll Kill You!" Verna repeated twice.

Then Fran opened a candy bar and took a bite and said, "Do you want this Verna?"

"You know I do," she replied.

"You can't have this one. Eat the one you saved from yesterday," Fran said in a teasing way.

"Are you for real?" Verna said looking puzzled.

"I'm just playing with you Girl. Here, you can have a whole new one."

"Thank you, Fran and can I have a bag of chips too?"

"Sure Ms. Piggy." And the two ate snacks and played cards.

Clarissa made a visit to see Fran. She had been in prison 12 months with a little more than a year left because the Warden received his payment of $15,000. Therefore, she is waiting to leave. Time was going by so fast. Three months had passed by since Fran had received the divorce papers from Bill and was not ready to sign them. The guard called Fran and told her she had a visit. She was trying to figure out who was her visitor so she went to the visiting room as saw a beautiful young lady waiting for her. She entered and waved to the guard to come over to where she was standing. Fran did not recognize any of the people in the room.

"Where's my visit?" she asked, "what's the person's name?"

The guard looked at the clipboard and said, "Clarissa Scott, you're at table eight." She walked over to her table and Clarissa stood up to greet her.

"Hello Francine," Clarissa in calm voice, "I'm Bill's fiancé."

"And what brings you here? I don't think we've met."

"Know I don't," said Clarissa, "I want to get right to the point. I know you're still married to Bill but I know he told you about me."

"He did," Fran replied, "but what do you want?"

"I want you to give him a divorce. He doesn't want you anymore so sign the Damn papers and get on with your life so we can get on with ours!"

"Is that what you two want me to do!?" Fran asked angrily, "did Bill send you to talk to me?"

"No, he did not," Clarissa replied, "I came to see you on my own. He also told me about you and how you're here for murder. He said you killed some drug addict."

Then Fran quickly asked, "Did he also tell you how I use to whip his Ass?"

"No, he did not."

"Well, I want you to give him a message for me. Tell him I will sign the papers and send them to him soon. And you, whatever your name is…you have the audacity to come in here and tell me what I should do. You're lucky I don't jump across this table and beat the lipstick off those pretty lips. But I don't want to bruise your pretty face. I want you to also give him this…" Fran spit in Clarissa's face.

Clarissa quickly wiped her face saying, "That was not very nice."

"It's not nice for you to come in here telling me what to do when I don't know you."

"Ok. I'll be leaving now," Clarissa said getting up to go.

"And don't bring your Monkey Ass back here either!"

"I'm so mad right now I could bust," Fran thought to herself.

And then she returned to her housing area. She was not happy that Clarissa came to her telling her to sign the divorce papers. But she wanted to do it for Bill and for herself. She wanted him to live his life and pick up what's left of hers.

The guard Ms. Downs was off the day Fran got attacked. Her son had gotten sick and another officer took her place. She was taking some clothes to the supply closet when three women came out of nowhere.

One of the women asked, "What's up now Sweetness?"

"Nothing," the frightened Fran said, "I don't want any trouble."

The woman Asia put a homemade knife to Fran's neck and said, "If you move, I'll Cut You."

"What do want?" Fran asked.

"I want you," Gina said rubbing Fran's cheek; she turned away, "don't fight it, I'll promise to be gentle." And she kissed Fran on the lips.

"Don't do this, I'll give you anything! Is it money you want?"

"No," Gina said, "it's you I want," as she unbuttoned Fran's shirt exposing her wonderfully formed breast.

The other women held her hand as Gina's lips found her breast. Then she pulled down her pants. She moaned from the Forbidden Pleasure. The woman put her face between Fran's thighs and began to pleasure her with her mouth. The women held Fran's breast as they pleasured themselves. The room seems to spin as Fran came to an explosion of orgasms that rocked her body like no other in her life.

Fran screamed with delight, "Oh My! You're Good!"

As Gina got up saying, "That's all I wanted."

Fran said, "I liked it so much that I'm not going to report this."

Fran is fixing her clothes and then said, "Oh, I forgot to tell you I'm HIV positive." Asia and Carla left the room very fast leaving Gina by herself.

As Gina looked like she had seen a ghost she asked, "How come you didn't tell me?"

"Bitch please!" Fran said as she laughed, "you 3 Psycho Bitches are going to come in here and take my Pussy hostage. However, I must say, that tongue of yours is immaculate. I hope you did not contract the virus, but if you did, I hope you don't spread it. Like I said, I'm not going to turn you in, but you should get tested in 90 days. That's called the window period.

You would know then if you have it or not. I know one thing; you won't put your mouth where it's not invited anymore. And another thing, Carla, and Asia will tell everybody that you are HIV positive when you might not be. I hope not, but if you are, you did it to yourself Sweetness. I want to say one more thing to you before I get back to work; lust dims the mind of consequences and makes you do some stupid things like you just did. I will sleep good tonight. Will you?" Gina just walked away like she lost her only friend.

As time went on, Gina became a nervous wreck. After that day in the Laundry Room, her thirst for Fran's affection came at a high price; one she wasn't willing to pay. Fran never told anyone what took place that day. The other two women never told anyone so that stayed in the walls of that room where Gina wanted it to stay. But she knew something might be lurking in her bloodstream that would rise up and take retribution for what she did to Fran.

A few weeks had passed since that day in the supply closet and Gina would even look at Fran if she didn't have to. But Fran would go out her way to speak to her. And when she did, the knife in her stomach would go in further. Gina would walk away miserable and afflicted.

Fran stuck her head into Gina's cell and said, "I'm not going to hold what you did to me against you because I think you hurt yourself more than me. I'm over it, you, on the other hand, are falling apart."

"What do you want?" Gina asked.

"I don't want anything," Fran said, "but if you need anything from me let me know. I want us to be friends; I forgive you and I know what you are going through. I'm here when you want to talk."

And Gina responded, "Why are you doing this to me?"

"What am I doing to you?"

"You're being all nice to me when I violated your space and now maybe, I caught something I can't get rid of."

"But you don't know if you got it, though," said Fran with her hand on Gina's shoulder. Gina is staring at Fran's hand on her arm.

"One thing I know is that you're not alone because God knows your heart. And maybe this is His way of getting your attention. And He knows you're a good person; you just wanted someone to notice you. And what you did to me was to make you feel good about yourself and make me feel bad about me. But think the opposite has occurred. But I feel more alive today than I did yesterday. I don't want to sound facetious when I say this, but I want to thank you for whatever you did to me. Because it made me appreciate all that I have and how fragile life is. And how it can be taken from you when you're least expect it. I want to start living instead of dying," she said as she grabbed Gina's hand, "and I want you to do the same thing. I once read this some place… *live your life today like you're going to die tomorrow.* What that was saying was…live your life to the fullest because tomorrow may never come." Gina started to cry; Fran hugged Gina and stroked her hair back gently trying to console a woman whose mental state fringes on the edge of collapse.

Fran made a call to Bill to tell him about Clarissa Scott's visit.

"Hello Bill, it's me calling to see how's everything going with you."

"Fine," he said.

"I met your Lady Friend the other day."

"Did you now," he said.

"Yes, I did and she informed me that she wants me to sign the divorce papers that you sent. I told her I would sign them and send them to you. Did you receive them yet?"

"I have not checked the mail."

"And I told her I would smear her lipstick across her pretty face and I spit on her too."

"That wasn't a nice thing to do."

"That's the same thing she said. I want you to tell her I apologize for acting the way I did. But tell her also to stay out business that don't concern her."

"I want you to know Fran, I had nothing to do with her coming to see you."

"It doesn't matter anyway; you got what you wanted," Fran said, "I must admit a jealous anger came over me and she was in my direct line of fire. My anger was fueled against you, and I took it out on her."

"But why be mad at me?"

"I know you know about a woman being scorned thing," said Fran, "well, I'm not. I don't have time to worry about what might have been; what we had is gone."

"I wouldn't say it's gone, but it has changed into something we can both agree to," Bill said, "I still love you, but we live in different worlds now."

And Fran said, "Once you give me that 2 million dollars in pocket change, you and Clarissa can go and enjoy that world that you spoke about. However, I want you to donate that money to a good cause like AIDS Awareness, its Research, and HIV medications for patients that can't afford it."

"Fran what's gotten into you? I think that is a wonderful idea. When did you become so charitable?"

"When I came to the realization that life would only give you what you ask for. And right now, I asking to be happy. If I give kindness, I receive kindness."

"And that is so true," Bill said, "I'll get right on that. Fran, I want to say it was a joy talking to you. You warmed my heart so much so that I will cherish your friendship for all times. In this life and those beyond." A tear rolled down Fran's cheek.

"Thank you, Bill."

Bill said to her humbly, "No…thank you. Goodbye and call again."

"I will," she said and hung the phone up feeling relieved and happy.

Verna even noticed the change in Fran's behavior. She was always nice to people. If she could not say something good about someone, she would not say anything. The women's crew treated Fran with respect. And if you treated her nice, she would do the same. And she had the Warden under her thumb, she had pizza brought in for her cell block. The women loved Fran and the younger ones started calling her "Mom Fran."

The prison did not serve cheesecake so, Fran got the Warden to start serving it to them and other menu changes. Like shrimp fried rice, Stromboli's and subs. In addition, she got the Warden to make other additions to the prison.

Fran started a Cosmetology class using her own money. She gave the prison one million dollars and the state matched it. Therefore, the prison had 2 million for equipment and construction. Fran did in 3 months, what no one had done in years. The Warden told Fran she was free to go, but she wanted to stay a little longer. The Warden said she could stay as long as she wanted. Gina took her test for HIV; the 90-window period was over. The results were to come back in two weeks. She would not eat because she worried about those test results.

Gina told Fran, "My life is over and no man would want me being HIV!"

"That's not True, they have support groups to help you work things out."

But Gina did not want to hear anything because she was in her darkest hour and her health was getting worse. She was losing weight, her hair looked a mess, and she wouldn't wash up. She let herself go. A woman who was once beautiful and had an exquisite figure was blowing away like the most fragile of flowers.

A week before her results were due, Gina started eating, started back talking, got hair done, polished her nails; she was on her way back to being that beautiful creature she had been at first.

Early that day Gina ate breakfast, went to the yard, played cards, talked with friends who asked her if she was alright. And she said she was. She ate her dinner, watched a little TV, talked to her cellmate and told her good night. Gina Davis not wanting to know the results of her test took an overdose of sleeping pills and killed herself. She was only 26-years-old.

After Gina's untimely death, Fran still wanted to know the results of her test. The doctor told Fran the test was NEGATIVE. Fran started to cry; it broke her heart that this young woman had to die because she told her to get tested. And she started to blame herself. *"I tried to talk to her but she would listen," Fran thought to herself.* After the body was released to the family Fran paid for Gina's funeral. A month after Gina died, Fran left Silent Hill Prison a free woman to live her life.

LESSON 27

Hands that Don't Want to Work Make You Poor,
But Hands that Work Hard Brings Wealth
(Proverbs 10:4)

Tony was on his way home from a meeting with a friend he had met 4 years ago when he was fooling around with Renay; his baby's mother. She was a stripping at the time and using drugs, but during that time Tony did not know. She had introduced the two men.

Renay said, "Tony this is my friend Bodabing aka Wild Turk." They called him that because he was from Turkey and he was crazy as hell.

Renay would buy drugs from Turk and when she did not have money he would give her credit or she would give him a good lap dance. And he told Tony if he wanted to make some fast money he needed to get in touch with him as soon as possible. But Tony never needed to call him because he had stop using drugs.

He then called Turk after he had blown $7,000 doing Cocaine with Jennifer. She would only sniff at first, but then Tony got her to start smoking it. Jennifer did not like getting high, but it was something to do when she wasn't doing anything. Tony told Turk he needed to invest some money and to get a quick return from it.

"What I suggest you do is decide what you want to invest in, whether it be guns, cocaine, heroin, prostitution, gambling, or stolen high-end cars. You can make money in all those enterprises," Turk said to Tony.

"But what I want to know, which one is the most lucrative?"

"Drugs," he answered, "I have connections in Istanbul, Turkey with people who are ready to do business."

"So, what kind of money are we talking?" Tony asked.

"It depends on how much we are going to deal and who will be our buyers. Or do I do all the drug transactions," Turk said while putting his hand on Tony's shoulder, "you provide your half and I'll provide my half of the money."

"How much money will I need to get this business proposition off the ground?" Tony asked him.

"You will need to get $150,000."

"What the hell…that's a lot of money," Tony said with shocking voice.

"It's nothing compared to what you're going to make," Turk quickly replied, "I'll match whatever you put up."

"So, your $150,000 and my $150,000 gives us $300,000. We'll then buy 20 Kilograms of Cocaine at $15,000 apiece. And I know we can get 3 free. Then we'll have 23 Kilos; then we will sell them at $25,000 apiece. And we'll make a profit of $200,750 and then we'll split it. Giving us over $100,000 apiece. We can make that in a week. I have people waiting right now who want to order."

"I'm so glad you called me," Turk said, "but I want to know how are we going get 20 Kilos of white sand back to the United States without getting busted by the Customs Agents or the Turkish Police. But if we do, we will never get out of jail."

"You're right about that," Tony said as he began to have second thoughts, "I don't know… I don't want to spend the rest of my life in prison. I'm only 28-years-old, and I'm not ready to retire."

"Don't worry, you're not going to jail," Turk said, "I want to share something with you since you and I are going to be business partners. I'm going to be straight with you, the night I met you was not by chance. I wanted to meet you because I knew your father had a lot of money and I also knew if he had it, you had it. Therefore, I told Renay to put the charms on you. I wanted to do business with you then, but I did not know where your head was. I also told Renay not to get you hooked on that Shit. The next thing I knew, that Shit had you in a choke hold and had you by the Balls. Are you using now?"

"No," Tony answered.

"Hey Man, don't lie to me; you're a Grown Ass Man. Do what you want to do, it's your money. Besides that, I don't see nothing wrong with doing a few lines now and then. I try not to get high on my own supply; that's why I stopped entirely."

"I'm trying to get my addiction under control also," Tony said, "and it's not easy; it's like using a bucket to get rid of water in a sinking boat. I stopped for a few years and then out of nowhere I started using again. It was like my addiction was working out getting stronger waiting on me to come back."

Turk said, "Listen, My Friend, if you put a lot into wanting to stop; you'll get a lot in return. And if you care a little, you're paid a little. I wanted you to work with me because your father's company has a refinery in Turkey. We can use Dark Water Oils as a front to bring our drugs over without fear of being caught. I'm not saying we can't get busted, but it's low risk. We also can use a private jet with Dark Water Oils Logo on it. I will need you to get me a job with the company to have our papers in order in case someone stops us to ask questions. That way we will have the answers for them."

"You have really thought this out," Tony said with a smile, "this is Fucking genius, Turk. You're Fucking 'CRAZY' like a fox."

"I do my best."

"How come you never did this without me?" Tony asked.

"Because I did not have your connections. You have Dark Water Oils, private jets, money, and the oil refinery in Turkey; perfect for my drug operation. Excuse me Tony for my selfish attitude, I meant OUR drug operation."

Tony then looked at Turk and asked, "How would the Cocaine be packed?"

"I'm glad you asked that. As you already know, we're only buying 20 Kilos'. Since we're buying that small amount, there is a coffee factory in the city of Bakirkoy. After we purchase the mal *(mal is a Turkish word for stuff)* we will then take the mal to the coffee factory where they're going to package it in coffee containers. Then it will be taken to Ataturk Airport for delivery to Dark Waters Oils Industries in the United States of America. It will then be put on your plane where you and I will take it back to the states. When do you want to leave?" Turk asked Tony.

"Next week," he answered, "I have to get the cash and make a few calls. Oh, and Turk, you never told me how the refinery played a part in all this."

"Let's work on this first and then we'll cross that bridge when we get there," Turk replied.

"Fine, I look forward to working with you."

"Same here," said Turk. And they shook hands and they went their separate ways.

The first thing Fran did when she got home from jail was take a shower in her own bathroom. Ms. Downs gave her a ride home; that was her last day at the prison. She quit her job to be Fran's personal assistant. Fran owned Bill's first house that she got in her first divorce settlement. It was a beautiful home. The love they had was long gone; if there ever was love between them. Even if Fran was home, her heart went out to the other women who may never see the street again. She thought of her old cellmate Verna; how she like to eat and how they loved each other as friends. And when she comes home; she will work for Fran as well.

She called Bill on his impending marriage to Clarissa and told him that she is a free woman. Also, that she has no ill feelings towards him or his bride to be. In addition, she told him she had met a man who cares about her and he does not care that she is HIV positive. He cares about the person she has become.

When the Warden Jake Swells asked Fran out she didn't know what to say so she just said yes. He had feelings for her the moment he read about her in the newspaper. He became confident that he would win her heart. He was the one who convinced her to donate the two million dollars to AIDS Research and Awareness.

After Fran was out of jail for a few weeks she became a champion for helping people and those who were sick. She would go to soup kitchens to donate food and money.

Fran called Tony, "Hello Son… how are you doing?"

"How are you doing Mom?"

"Fine and free," she replied.

"Oh, you're out?"

"Yes indeed, yes I am."

"Good for you Mom. And how are you really doing?"

"What do you mean?" Fran asked.

"You know," he said.

"I don't know…tell me."

"Your illness," he responded in a soft voice.

"Oh, that? It's called HIV. Don't be afraid to say it. I'm learning to live with it. All I have to do is eat healthy, take my meds and pray. And how are you really doing? Are you still messing with that Dope?"

"No Mother," he answered.

"Don't give me that 'No Mother Crap'. Look, Son, I'm not here to pull you down; I want to pull you up. You have been there and done that so why are you going back? And that's not the worst of it, you have two people you're taking down with you. So, what do you have to say for yourself? And please don't drag that poor woman down with you. If you continue the way you're going, you will have nothing. And I will find you living under a bridge, fighting with some bum about who is going to get the last sip of wine or whose turn it is to sleep with Lucy tonight." Fran is pushing for her son and pleading with him.

He then asked her, "Are you finished?"

"Yes, I am," Fran said.

"I'm not going to let Jennifer down or my son. I owe it to them to protect them."

"From what?" Fran asked, "did you protect Jennifer from getting high with you? No…so, who are you protecting them from? If you don't get yourself together some man will have her, will appreciate her and respect her for the person she is."

"But I love her!" Tony yelled.

"Well, act like it then!" she said raising her voice, "I told Jennifer to stop using those drugs and divorce you before you destroy her. And maybe by her leaving you, you'll put your life back on track."

"I'm going to take your advice, Mom."

"I hope so Son because I don't want to see you down and out. I want you to know one thing; if you fall, I'll be here to help you up."

"Thank you, Mom and I love you."

"I love you too Son."

When Fran got off the phone from talking to Tony she felt a deep sadness for Jennifer and Little Mark. Therefore, she wept in silence. Her time in jail taught her a great deal about family and friends. That she should love them with all that she has. *She thought about what someone once said, let him that can love do so because hate has no place where love is.*

It was cold that afternoon when Jennifer left to go shopping for her family. She and Tony had been married almost 5 years. And two of the last had not been that good. Tony wasn't home half the time and when he was he was asleep and left her to care for the baby who was 5-years-old. Jennifer went inside the market. It was this one fellow who always went out his way to be nice to her.

He walked up to her and said, "What brings a lady as beautiful as you to a place like this and can I be of service to you?"

"I'll let you know when I do."

"Please do," he said. Then he would follow her around the entire time from a distance.

Jennifer notices the fellow following her from a distance so, she waved to him to come to her and he did.

"Where is all the cheese?" she asked.

"It's gone? I'll go in the back and get some." He backs up to go get the cheese while still watching Jennifer.

Then she said, "You better watch where you're going before you hurt yourself. I'll be here when you get back." He came back a few minutes later with the cheese.

"Thank you, Mr. Travis," she said as she read his name tag, "I will remember you."

"I hope so because I will remember you," he responded, "can I call you?"

"I don't think so; I'm married."

"Are you happily?"

"That's none of your business Travis."

"So, I assume you're not."

"I'll see you another time; bye now," and she walked way, "and don't follow me." She finished her shopping and she was putting her bags in the car and someone grabbed the bag; it was Travis again.

"Didn't I tell you not to follow me!"

"I'm sorry, but you are so beautiful," he said as he put the bags in the car.

"Thank you. Do you work here full time or part time?"

"Part-time," he answered.

"Are you a stalker in your other part time job?"

"Noooo I don't do that."

"I can't tell; you followed me the entire time I was in the store," she said to him as she got in her car and he's still looking, "and I'm not tipping you either!" And she pulls off.

Jennifer returned home two hours later. She entered the house and yelled to Tony to tell him she was home and asked him to help her with the groceries. She still did not get an answer after calling his name several times. So, she began to search the rooms. She went into Little Mark's room and he was asleep. Then she checked the bedroom, he was not there. Then she checked the basement and he wasn't there either. Finally, she checked the entire house and there was no sign of Tony.

"His car is still in the driveway so he must be still here," she thought to herself, "I don't think he would leave the baby here by himself." Jennifer got tired of looking for him so, she set down and turned on the TV to the watch her soaps.

An hour had passed since returning to the house and she was getting sleepy. She dozed off for a minute and when she woke up, Tony was standing over her. She immediately screamed and with a quick reaction the remote control found the side of Tony's face as it broke into pieces. Tony then grabbed his face in pain.

"What's the hell is wrong with you!"

Then she said, "What the hell is wrong with you scaring me like that?"

"I'm sorry," he said holding his head.

"You heard me calling you so, why didn't you answer me?" she asked looking very angry, "and why are you in your underwear sweating like the running man? I know why I couldn't find you. You were in the Damn closet again getting high. And that explains why you are sweating, all paranoid and out of your mind."

"You want to join me?" he asked.

"Where? In the closet? No thanks," she said as she put a soft cloth on Tony's cut, "I don't want to live like this anymore. And I don't want to use anymore either. And when I did, it was not a good feeling after I came down. I know that kind of life will only lead to institutions and death."

"I know," Tony said, "I'm going to stop."

"When?" she responded, "when you're broke and homeless. Or when you lose me or whichever comes first. And besides that, you have a son to take care of. He depends on you and me. And I'm not going to let him down. And I'm not going to let you let him down. I want you to promise me something?"

"And what would that be?" Tony asked.

Then Jennifer looked him in his eyes and said, "If you use any more drugs anywhere; in the car, the closet, the bathroom or across the world and I find out, I'm going to divorce you and take you for everything you got left. All that you don't give to the drug dealer."

Then he responds, "You would do that to me?"

"Try me! And I won't be ignored this time Tony. I'm serious about this and I hope you are too. I waited for you the first time to get things back in order and I won't do it again. Don't I have the right to be happy in my life? I only have one life to live and I want to live it. You were born with everything; caring parents to provide you with the best of everything. I have good parents also and I don't want to disappoint them being on drugs. I don't want you to disappoint yours for a second time. I don't want to be with someone who wants to see me hurt. And you hurt me when you gave me drugs. I know you didn't mean too, but I didn't like who we were becoming."

"I'm sorry for everything I took you through," Tony said as bent down on one knee and took her hand and gently kissed it, "I will never mistreat you ever again."

As he looked up into her eyes a tear fell and landed on his cheek. He then stood up and embraced his wife.

LESSON 28

Those Who Talk About Others Tell Secrets,
But Those Who Can Be Trusted Keeps Things to Themselves

The two weeks had passed since Tony last talked to Turk. He had set up everything; the job passes, got authorization to use the company jet, and rounded up the $150,000 from a family friend. Who knew if anything happened to the money or Tony got busted, Bill would pay out the loss for him. So, he thought, but only time would tell.

Turk told Tony they would leave JF Kennedy Airport at 6pm and it would take 10 hours without stopping. Therefore, they would arrive at Ataturk Airport at 3am American time.

Tony and Turk took the trip to Turkey where they met two men at the airport and they spoke in Turkish. And one man said, "Merhaba" which means hello. The men told them they would take them to the "Mal" which means stuff. And they could discuss how much they wanted to buy once they got to the city of Bakirkoy.

Once they entered the city, the streets were packed with people going about their everyday lives. The man that was driving, drove well as he darted in and out of traffic barely missing an old man on a bike.

The old man on a bike yelled, "Baksana Ondne!" Which means "Look Out" as he turned the corner. The driver then stopped at a hotel.

"OK we're here," Turk said, "I will go in and get two rooms just in case we have to stay for a few days. Something may go wrong, we have to be prepared, anything can happen."

As the two men went to the front desk the Bell Hop said, "Can I take your bags?" Each man had one suitcase. One contained the $300,000 and the other contained two guns.

Turk told the man, "No thank you, I'll manage," and then he said to the clerk, "two rooms, one night."

"Okay, that would be $200.00." Turk paid with 2 American $100.00 bills.

"Thank you," he said. And the two men received their keys and walked to the elevator. They went to the 2nd Floor; the rooms were right next to each other.

"I'm going to take a shower and get something to eat; I'll meet you in an hour downstairs in the lobby," Turk said, "I have to make phone calls and make sure everything is ready to go. Oh, and you hold the money." He opened the suitcase; it held the two guns and he gave one to Tony.

"I'm not good with these," he said.

Turk quickly responded to him, "If someone tries to take the money…SHOOT THEM!"

"SHOOT THEM!" Tony repeated.

"That's right! If you don't, you will be dead!!! And I'ma be out of a $150,000," Turk said as he turned to go in his room, "I'll see you in a few." Then he closed his door.

Tony went to his room, sat down at the mini bar and took a drink. As he was drinking he thought about Jennifer, the baby, and the risk he was taking coming to another country to buy drugs. *"I must be insane," he thought as he chuckled to himself and continued to drink.* He then laid back in the chair for a nap after the long ride. They stopped once to refuel, so, this rest was well needed.

He slept for 20 minutes and then got up and took a hot shower. But he put the same close on because he did not plan on staying long. After a quick shower, he was ready to go down and get something to eat and meet Turk.

Tony left his room and walked down a long hallway. He forgot which way the elevator was as he walked with the 300,000 in the briefcase and a gun in his waist. He felt safe with a weapon. But he knew if he was confronted with danger, he would Shit in his pants, drop the gun, and give the money away just as long as they didn't kill him. He walked passed a door that was open, he noticed two men beating another man. Therefore, he quickly kept walking until he came to an exit that led to the stairs. He began running down them to the 1st Floor scared and paranoid that the men he saw were chasing him because he saw their faces. The men never saw him because they were too busy beating up that poor man. So, when Tony reached the lobby hyperventilating and trying to catch his breath, a man passing by asked him was he alright. He could not breathe that well, but he managed to say that he was alright. But that was a lie. Most people would believe any lie, either because they wanted to believe it was true or because they feared it was.

Tony was far from alright because he had just seen something that he intuition connected with. And the fear that overtook him was real and he felt it. He then walked into the lobby expecting to see Turk but he didn't. He looked all over the place and he was nowhere to be found. He then became more nervous than ever, pacing back and forth. And then out of the corner of his eye, he saw a limping man emerging from the exit coming from the stairs. It's Turk and he's been hurt.

"What happen to you?" Tony exclaimed.

"I ran into some old friends."

Then Tony said, "If your friends did this, I would hate to see what your enemies do to you. I saw a guy getting beat up on the 2nd Floor. That was you! And who were those guys?"

"I owe them money," Turk answered.

"Well, it's a good thing I held on to ours because they would have taken it. And where is your gun?" Tony asked.

"They took it," Turk said grabbing his stomach.

"Are you ready to do this?" Tony asked, "we can put this off until tomorrow."

Turk then responds, "We can't! We have to get back to the States as soon as we can. I told them I would have their money by 9am tomorrow."

"How much do you owe them?" Tony asked.

"$200,000," he answered.

"I want to know one thing," Tony said as his face turned red, "why did you bring me all the way over here in your country where you owe people money. What kind of Turkish Asshole are you!? I had to be out of my mind listening to you!"

"It's not too late, we can still do it!" Turk said.

"How? You may have compromised the whole Fucking deal! Who knows those guys may be watching us right now, planning to take you out with your own gun and me because I'm with you. I think I should bail out now!" Tony yelled.

"No! We can still do it! Please believe me!" Turk said as he pleaded with him not to abandon the plan.

"I think we should change the way we're going to do business. I'll make the tradeoff for the drugs and you watch my back," Tony said.

"I will call the Connection and tell them to meet you at the coffee factory and I'll back you up." Turk made the call and the Connect agreed to the rendezvous at 4pm.

Turk and Tony returned to their rooms. Tony is still suspicious about the men who beat the mousse out of Turk's hair and he wanted to change a few details about the plan.

The two men left the hotel in separate cars; Turk left first. Tony left 10 minutes later. The reason they left at different times were to throw anyone off that was following them. One of the men arrived at the coffee factory at 3:48pm. He had his gun on his waist and the money in the briefcase for the transaction. The man with the money waited patiently outside of the warehouse; then a black Mercedes Benz pulled up. Two men got out of the car and walked towards the men that were waiting.

"Tony? I presume," one of the men said.

"Mal-Nerde," he said. *(which means do you got the stuff)*

"I see you speak Turkish."

"It's me, Turk."

The man then asked, "What happened to your America friend?"

"He's around."

"That's very good Para-Nerde?" he asked Turk. *(which means do you got the money)*

"Every dime," Turk answered, "we have agreed to a price of $300,000 for 23 Kilograms."

"And that's what it will be," the man said whose name was Hansa Vardor. He will a major drug supplier in Turkey.

Hansa reached into the trunk and pulled out a black duffle bag with 23 bricks of Cocaine and passed it to a smiling Turk.

Turk said to Hansa, "There is only one thing left to do and the business deal is over."

"And what's that, My Friend?"

"Is to test it and make sure it's not milk powder or flour."

"Test all you want; I stand behind my product," Hansa said with an attitude.

"And I stand behind my money," Turk said while reaching inside the duffle bag to randomly grab one of the Kilos.

He then pulled a knife out and cut a slit in the package. He scooped a little to taste; with one finger, he put the powdered substance on his gums and in his mouth. He felt a numbing sensation.

"I can't feel my tongue and niss is good Shit! And quickly gave Hansa the money." The man took the money, got in his car, and pulled off.

Then Turk went inside the factory where he met a woman named Isabelle and a man named Benjamin who was American. They would package the cocaine in coffee boxes, make order forms and invoices for shipping to the airport for loading on the company plane. The man and women were paid $500 apiece for their work. The two would also be the one's shipping it to the Ataturk runway.

Tony stayed away from the drug deal because those two men did follow him for 6 blocks in a cab because they thought he was Turk. He and Turk traded clothes back at the hotel hours ago. The men that were following stopped him.

"Wild Man, you'd better have that..." But they stopped short of saying 'the money' because they did not recognize Tony and told him "Sorry" and went on their way.

Tony told Turk to meet him at the airport after he seals the deal with Hansa. Turk waited for Isabelle and Benjamin to put the Cocaine in boxes and wrap them in plastic so they don't come apart during shipping. After they were done, he followed them to the airport to make sure everything went as planned. He also followed the delivery van through grueling traffic. He almost lost them 3 times darting in and out a gauntlet of cars.

As the van entered an intersection the driver noticed a road block. He stopped the van and told Turk what the situation was. Isabelle got out too and she added to the conversation with excitement that they are checking cars and vans.

"And we have a van!" she said, "We're going to jail…and I have kids! I'm going to jail!" Isabelle yells I'm going to jail repeatedly.

She began to talk louder and became very hysterical. Then Benjamin smacked her across the face and told her to pull herself together before she blows everything. Then she calmed down and went back to the van.

"That was a good thing you did by smacking her," Turk told Ben, "keep an eye on her; she might crack at the wrong time. And then we will all go to prison."

Benjamin then went back to the van. Isabelle is a nervous wreck and close to a breakdown.

Benjamin said, "Listen, Women, if you don't calm down I'm going to Fuckin' Shoot You! You Fuckin' pull yourself together right now!"

They are now getting closer to the checkpoint. Benjamin slams on the breaks and then stops the van and jumps out. He goes around to the passenger's side and opens the door. He grabs Isabelle by the arm, then pulls her out of the van; and takes her back to Turk's car.

"Let her get in here with you! Because if she stays with me, she's going to Fuck us all with her clothes on!" He puts her in the back seat and she calms down.

"I'm sorry about that," she said. But Turk said nothing.

Benjamin goes back to the van; he gets in and then moves forward. The police stop the van and he provides his license and driving credentials. He also showed him the delivery forms for coffee. The police inspected his license and papers and told him to move on. The police did the same thing with Turk's car but he was not driving. The man that was driving provided his driving credentials also.

Once the vehicles got through the checkpoint Turk felt good that they did. But they had to make it off the grounds and not to mention getting the cargo onto the plane. There was airport security all over the place.

They arrived at their destination 20 minutes later. They entered the gate and Benjamin presented his paperwork to security. They even had drug sniffing dogs, but they could not detect the drugs because of the coffee that surrounded it.

After security checked it, the authorization was given for the cargo to be put on the Dark Water Oils Industries Jet which was private. Therefore, Benjamin immediately delivered the packages to the plane. Meanwhile, Turk had to wait for Tony because he had the documents to board the private jet. Then Tony finally arrived.

"What the hell took you so long?" Turk asked.

"I ran into your old friends. They did not beat my Ass like they did to you," Tony responded.

"So, what did they want?"

"They wanted the money you owe them Shit for brains. I wonder how you made it this far."

"What do you mean?" he asked.

"Never mind," Tony said, "I want to get out of here."

The two went to get on the plane and when they got there the pilots were ready to go. Everything had been loaded onto the plane. The pilot called the tower for clearance to take off. Permission was then granted. And then they took off with 23 Kilos of Cocaine that they would sell to other dealers. In turn, they would then cut the drugs for street sales.

The cycle of death and violence continues. But the men did not know the lives they will affect with this poison. They plan to distribute to people who will become habitually addicted to the lifestyle that they will have a love-hate relationship with. They want to let it go but they can't, so, they think. The person must invest in order to get a return. Just like the bankers on Wall Street; money is invested and they hope that money is returned. But if a person is held down by drugs, you must invest in your life and life will be returned to you. Because it is the natural order of things. If you put a lot in, you will get a lot back. If you put in a little, a little will come back.

The Dark Water Oils Industries Jet landed at JFK Airport 12 hours later. The drugs were unloaded by employees of the airport and it passed through customs without a problem.

Tony called someone to pick up the shipment of drugs to take them to one of the company warehouses. Where he and Turk will pick it up for delivery to the buyers that put their orders in to become hunters of people's lives. The state where Tony lived had the largest enlisted drug markets in the United States. In many of the neighborhoods cocaine, heroin, marijuana and PCP are sold openly and are available 24 hours a day; partially on the West side and most pronounced. And the people living in these places are living at or below the poverty line. And most of the citizens are unemployed or on welfare. Dropout rates of children are high. Drug arrest and substance abuse are at alarming rates. Most of the dealers are freelancers with their own supplies and responsible for their profits and losses. The dealers are rarely fronted drugs. But sometimes they are given drugs to sell and are allowed to pay for it later. They sell for their own profits and generally are fighting for competition for a small number of addicted daily users. Addicts who always try to negotiate the price down. Most of these people who try to negotiate come from all walks of life. Then you have prostitutes' willing to do anything to get the drug of their choice.

Tony did not realize the drugs he was about to sell would destroy many lives in its wake. The road of drugs is long and hard. Many will go into this not considering the consequences and some will not return to a sound mind and remain desolate and barren of their senses. Tony knows what drugs do to you because he's been there. And he knows the pitfalls. Once you pick up a drug, you might now put it down because you might die with it in your hand.

Tony and Turk picked up the 23 Kilos of Coke from the warehouse. Where company supplies were kept like oil drums, fork lift trucks, and company cars. Turk called buyers and sold 10 Kilos in less than 3 hours. The men made $250,000. Tony could not believe his eyes as he counted the drug proceeds. They have 13 Kilos left to sell. Five buyers reneged on their offer to purchase 2 bricks apiece. Turk would have to locate new customers and fast.

He located a guy named Sterling Sticks who was a small-time dealer who was gang affiliated, but not gang directed. Turk did not know Sterling at all, but a friend told him he was a good customer with $50,000 to spend on some Good Shit. So, Turk gave him a call. Ring, Ring, Ring.

"Hello?"

"This is Turk…can I speak to Sterling?"

"Yo What's up, speaking?"

"Can you meet me on the outside of Arica's Café in town?

"Sure. What time."

"Tomorrow at 4 o' clock."

"OK, see you then."

"OK, later." Tony Told Turk of his plans to meet Sterling at Arica's Café tomorrow at 4 o'clock.

"Tony, watch out for any funny business because a lot of gangs live around where you guys are going to meet and take your gun. I'll back you up if I can," Turk suggested to Tony.

Sterling called Turk back and told him he wants 2 more Kilos and he'll bring $100,000 cash. And Turk agreed.

The two men knew the dangers of dealing drugs and that they could lose their lives because of their greed and the ability to dismantle families. Families who built stable households that took years are destroyed.

Women sometimes are pulled into a vortex of pain and sadness, which they cannot escape. Death, disease, and prison become their passage. All Queens must lift themselves out of the pits of despair and loneliness because they are the birth of life. And when they are heavy with the fruit of life within their womb, for they are a wonder. For they give off a deep mystery that no one can explain. The more illegal the behavior, the more the woman has to lose.

The next day, Tony went to meet Sterling Sticks at Arica's Café on Fashionett Street where two days earlier 2 people were murdered from a drug deal gone bad. But this information was foreign to these men, who would find out later that this neighborhood was a hotbed for violence and gang activity. Where gunshots are commonplace and anyone could get hit by stray bullets.

Sterling told Turk he would be waiting in a red hat and black pants, and he would be sitting by himself at a table in the corner of the café. The men parked 2 blocks away from the café so Sterling would not know what they arrived in. They walked down towards Arica's Café with a briefcase with the bricks inside.

"Do yall guys need anything? We got the Best Shit in town," a man on the street said to them." Both men shook their heads no.

Then the man said to them, "You're in a war zone because gangs are fighting for turf or position. Many dealers work the same corner. They're claiming something that's not theirs and will die to protect it."

Tony and Turk did not respond. However, they walked faster taking in consideration what the man said. Nevertheless, they got to the café safely. When they walked in the door, Sterling was sitting in the corner and he waved at them. He did not know if they were the men he was supposed to meet, but he took a chance. Turk noticed the red hat and waved back. The man in the corner looked menacing and sneaky. Tony felt a chill of apprehension and an urge to turn away, but he continued to greet the man.

Sterling stood up to shake both their hands. Turk extended his hand and he shook it. However, Tony did not extend his.

Sterling said, "I like to shake a man's hand that I'm doing business with."

"I want to do, what we came here to do," Tony said, "I don't trust you."

"Is that so?"

"No," he responded.

"Well, let us conduct business before things get out of hand," Sterling said as he shows Turk and Tony the money. They then showed him the Cocaine.

"It looks good; close it," he said. Turk asked him if he would like to sample it first.

He responded, "I trust you guys."

He then called the waiter that was standing a few feet away. Who came over and asked the men if they wanted anything to drink and then put a gun to Turk's head. And Sterling pulled a gun from under the table and pointed it at Tony.

"If you move, I'll paint the floor with Your Fucking Brains! Try Me!" he said. And the waiter took the briefcase from Turk with the gun still pointed at his head.

Turk then said, "This is bad business."

Sterling told the men, "You guys made a bad mistake trusting someone you did not know. The other mistake was, you let me pick the meeting spot. I'm going to let you two live since you gave me 4 Kilos of Cocaine for nothing," then he put his hand in Turks jacket and took his gun, "now get out of here before I change my mind!"

The two men got up and walked away.

Tony said, "You really got us Fucked this time Turk."

Ask they walked back towards the car they heard gun shots. So, they started running as Sterling shot 2 more times in the air as he pulled off in his car with $100,000 worth of cocaine.

Tony and Turk reached their car tired and mad, but happy to make it out alive. Even though they were $100,000 in the red they still had 9 Kilos left.

LESSON 29

The Treasure that Awaits Your Attention is On a New Road
Find that Road and You Will Find that Treasure

Fran is still upset that Gina killed herself and *she thought to herself, "What a waste, a young woman with her whole life ahead of her had to die young. Her dreams will never be realized; her children will never be born, and the work she was supposed to perform will go undone. Her family will miss her for the person she was and all who loved her. A sad chapter in one's life who had so much promise."*

Verna on the other hand will leave Silent Hill Prison a new woman because of Fran's friendship and wisdom. Friendship and wisdom that she would take with her to enrich her life to become a good mother to her unborn children. And when they arrive, she would teach them that life will only give them what they ask for. And they must earn their place in this world. Most importantly, they can do anything if their heart and mind are in the right place and they believe in a Higher Power. Because He makes all things possible and without Him we are nothing. Knowing we must cling to His everlasting love.

The day Verna was released from jail her friend was waiting for her at the front gate. The limo pulled up a few minutes before she came out.

"Hey, Stranger!" Fran yelled to the smiling Verna who ran to the car to hug her. As the two women hugged each other they cried a combination of tears, joy, pain, and happiness.

Verna loved Fran because she told her that she would make sure she was alright. She even had a job waiting for her. They had a friendship that would last a lifetime. And what God joins together, no man can tear apart.

"I thought you would've forgotten about me once you went home," Verna said with her hand over her mouth.

She was not trying to show her true emotions. Because she had been let down so many times in her life. So now, she had someone who truly cared for her.

Fran said, "Oh, you thought I would forget about you."

"Yes," she answered.

"Not! You're my new friend. I told you I would set you up once you got out of this Shit Hole," Fran said to her.

"Thank you," she said.

"I know you're hungry so, where do we go to eat?" Fran asked.

"I don't know, I don't care wherever you take me," Verna quickly replied, "But I don't want to go to one of those fancy restaurants where the plates look pretty with nothing on them. I want some fried chicken, French fries, and an iced tea."

"That sounds good, let's go. Get in."

"I'm going home in style," Verna said as shuts her door and yells out the window, "so long Bitches!"

Fran said, "Don't do that, you might jinx yourself. Just leave and hope you never come back."

"I'm not coming back here," she said.

"I hope not," Fran said as she tapped the driver to pull off.

They drove away never to look back at this dark lonely place. The two women arrived at Aunt Bumby's Restaurant *(a soul food place)* who served the best-fried chicken in the city.

A woman named Leana greeted them, "Welcome to Aunt Bumby's; may

I take your order?"

"Yes, I would like fried chicken with fries, coleslaw, and an iced tea."

"And what would you like?" the women asked turning to Fran.

"I'll have what she's having," Fran said as Leana wrote down their orders.

"Is it here or to go?" the woman asked.

"We will be eating here; this place is real nice."

Verna asked, "How did you hear about this place?"

"My business partner Linda Cates used the catering service for a party she had for me when I got out. The food was delicious and the peach cobbler is to die for," As a matter of fact, "excuse me Ms. Leana, can you add two orders of peach cobbler?"

"Large or small?" she asked.

"Large because my friend here has a huge appetite and after she tastes that cobbler, she'll want the whole pan."

Then Leana said, "It's for sale."

Ten minutes later their food was ready and Leana gave the ladies their orders and they started eating. Verna was eating her food fast.

"Slow down Ms. Piggy," Fran said. Verna just looked at her and continued eating.

She managed to say between chews, "I just got through doing 3 years in prison. I will not slow down until it's gone."

"Well, enjoy yourself."

"I intend too. And if you don't finish that I will," Verna said while drinking her iced tea.

"I told you this food is to die for so, don't make me kill you," Fran said biting into her chicken.

Verna said to her as she busted out laughing, "You're one Sick Bitch!"

They both laughed and continued eating. Verna ate everything on her plate including a piece of chicken that Fran did not eat. Ten minutes later, they were finished and preceded to leave. Fran thanked Leana for a fine meal and paid her for their food.

The driver opened the door for the women and they got in the Limo.

"I can get used to this," said Verna.

"Do you have somewhere to live?" Fran asked getting straight to the point.

"Not really."

"What does *not really* mean? You do or you don't," Fran said.

"No," she answered, "I don't have my place anymore."

"Well, you can stay with me. I need a maid to clean up and do housework. Do you want the job?" Fran asked her.

"I sure do."

"Can you cook?"

"I sure can."

"Welcome aboard," said Fran.

"I won't let you down," Verna said as she started to cry again.

"Stop that Crying Shit!" Fran said with an attitude, "if you cry all the time, what the hell is the baby going to do?"

"I'm sorry. Nobody's been this nice to me ever."

"Well, times have changed. I'll pay you $500.00 a week and your room and board are free. All that I ask, is that you open a bank account and save your money. And then maybe someday you can get your own place.

But until then, you can stay as long as you want. Just keep my house clean."

"Thank you, Fran."

"It's nothing, you're my friend Silly," she said with a smile, "and don't you start that Crying Shit. If I can help you, I will. Besides that, I'm rich."

"You are that," Verna agreed, "I may not want to leave after I move in."

"This is a sweet deal so don't blow it," said Fran.

"I won't."

The Limo pulled into Fran's driveway.

"Oh, My! Oh, My! Oh, My! It's beautiful! Who lives here with you?" Verna asked her.

"Nobody but you as of right now. I always wanted another live-in maid."

"What happened to the one you had?"

"I fired her."

"For what?" Verna asked.

"For having a baby with my husband."

"Oh, that was wrong."

"It was," Fran responded, "I beat her Ass Good! And that was the reason I divorced him the first time. Actually, this was his house. He gave it to me or did I take it?" Fran used her key to open the door.

Verna stepped in and said, "I'm not leaving! Ever!"

"You might change your mind after you have been here awhile because sometimes I have mood swings. I wasn't always nice as I am now. I can be a real Bitch. So, don't pop the champagne just yet Sweetie."

"I'll deal with it," Verna said.

"Alright then…I warned you," Fran replied, "I'm having company over later."

"Who's coming over?" she asked.

"Jake Swells."

"The Warden? I knew you two had something going on. He was giving you too much freedom. He was letting you do anything you wanted."

Then Fran looked at Verna and said, "Money is Power! That's the reason I did want I wanted."

The doorbell rang and Fran went to open it, but stopped and said, "Oh, I forgot, I have a maid." Then she looked at Verna and pointed to the door.

"Oh, you want me to open it?"

"You are the maid, aren't you?" Verna looked at Fran and quickly opened the door.

When she opened it, a tall Black female was standing in the doorway; it was Ms. Downs.

"Hello, Fran… hello, Verna. They let you out?" Ms. Downs asked as she hugged Verna.

"They couldn't keep me forever."

"The hell if they can't…while you're out, just keep yourself out of trouble. And don't give them a reason to put your Ass back in. Because you know your cell is probably still open."

"I know that's right," Verna said. Ms. Downs then handed Fran some paperwork from her lawyer.

Verna got herself all settled in her new home and got prepared to work. Fran took her upstairs and showed Verna her room, it was nice and cozy. And she started crying again.

"Please don't do that."

"Do what?"

"Cry."

"But I can't help it."

"OK, go ahead and cry. You're nothing but a Big Cry Baby anyway."

"I know."

"I have a gift for you, but I'll wait until tomorrow to give it to you," said Fran, "I had enough of your raining eyes."

Fran and Verna went back downstairs and Ms. Downs is sitting at the table and asked, "Who wants to play some Spades and lose some money?" Frans looks at Verna and said, "She's talking to me because she knows you're flat broke. She wants to reel me in."

"Do you want to play with us?"

"I don't have any money," Verna said looking apologetic.

"It's alright, I'll give you an advance."

"That will be fine. I'll take your money and yours too Ms. Downs. I'm the Spades Champ."

"I'll see about that," Ms. Downs said quickly.

The two women joined Ms. Downs at the table. They played cards and talked about old times. They played all morning, enjoying each other's company passing money around. Verna was lucky, she won $100.00.

"I think I'll paint the town 'RED' tonight. Do me some dancing and let some strange man take advantage of me. Because me so Horney!" Verna said.

"You're a Sick Bitch," Fran said to her.

"I know I'm Crazy. What about you?"

"I'm alright."

"So, you think," Verna responded, "you're a Crazy Bitch with money."

"Who you calling Bitch? I can call you a 'Bitch' but you don't call me one," said Fran.

"Now, I know you're Crazy; I love you, though."

Ms. Downs said, "I have to pick up my son from school so, I'll see you two later. Bye." Then she leaves.

The three came from different places in the world but they had one thing in common. They all had struggles that they would use as stepping stones to something greater. The three women gave a part of themselves to each other. Whatever piece that was missing from the puzzle of their lives they found it in one another. It's the stuff that makes life worth living and gives you that push to make your dreams come true.

Then Verna decided to go shopping for an outfit for her big night on the town because Fran wanted to be alone later with her friend.

Two hours later, Verna returned to Fran's house and then she took a shower without some women looking at her Tits asking can she touch them. And she would say yes. Truthfully speaking, that's how she got turned out in the first place.

There's woman in Silent Hill Prison that Verna still has strong feelings for, who she plans to be with when she gets out. But for right now, she would keep that information to herself. The woman that Verna has feeling for is the one that Fran caught her with in the cell. Is it wrong to be with the same sex? The love that they have transcends beyond the sex organs into a place of peace with oneself. And no one can change a love such is that. We as people look for love that goes beyond what we've been taught. For a love, such as this will make men forfeit their lives and the person they love. Jealousy and lust create carnage; for it is a recipe for death. If a person loves you more than themselves, it would be wise to sever your relationship with them. And it must be done with ease because sudden separation can result in a mental breakdown with partial personality discomfort. In short, the person may go crazy and tell the person that they love; if they can't have them, nobody will. Then the person is then hurt or even killed for the sake of love.

Verna went out to enjoy herself at a club called 'The Snake Pit' where she danced her heart out and got wasted. Also, she met a man at the bar.

"Can I take you home?" he asked.

"No, you can't," she answered in a slurred voice pointing her finger at him, "I don't like men; I like women," she said in her inebriated state. The man began to rub Verna's thigh under the bar.

"I...I...I see you have a hand problem, if you touch me again I will break your Fucking fingers!" Quickly the man removed his hand as she became loud and belligerent.

Verna was normally a quiet woman but now has become an acholic induced monster.

Verna yelled out, "I came here to party! I've been in jail for 3 years; I want to party!" Then she got up on the bar and started dancing like a stripper.

"Come down before you fall and hurt yourself!" the bartender yelled. Then suddenly she took a step to the left and fell behind the bar with a crash. The bartender was laughing so hard and so was everybody else.

She pops up embarrassed and yells, "I'm alright! And all of yall can kiss my White Ass!" She's having a bad time right now.

Fran on the other hand, was having a good time with her friend Jake Swells who brought her some roses when he came to see her. He arrived about 9pm. Fran opened the door.

"Hello Stranger," the smiling man said to the beautifully dressed women.

"Hello Handsome," she responded.

"Are you ready to go?"

"Yes, let me get my coat," she answered. They left to go to dinner and a concert in the city.

The two were chauffeured around town as they sipped champagne and laughed about old times.

Fran looked Jake in his eyes and asked, "Can you truly love me with my disease?"

"Yes, I can," he answered as he lightly kissed her lips, "my feelings for you goes beyond your circumstance. I do believe we can build a meaningful relationship."

"A lot of women who have my illness fears that no man will love them truly because he fears he would be infected. Meaning, he would waste away and die alone. I don't know what tomorrow will bring, but I thank God I'm here today." Fran took Jakes hand in hers.

"The future belongs those who believes in the beauty of tomorrow."

"I agree with that; I'm sorry that Gina didn't believe. I still think of her often. I had to call her parents to tell them that their little girl had passed away. I hate that part of my job. I want to inform those who are ill, live your life because all is not lost."

Fran and her date enjoyed their night on the town as they danced the whole time. She would not let HIV rob her of her happiness. She had a right to be happy and a man that would love her despite her illness. And she would find him in an unlikely place; the state prison. It's not where you find your mate, it's how.

Jake told Fran he did not care where she came from. And he was happy she came into his life because his wife died of cancer two years before. He was lonely and wanted companionship which was needed to make his life complete.

The love birds concluded their date. Fran's driver dropped her off first. She embraced Jake and took him in her arms as he whispers in her ear.

"Your strength that keeps you, will keep us also." Then he gently kissed her on the forehead and she thanked for a wonderful night.

Then Fran thought to herself, "I look forward to more to come as our love blossoms to the greatest of all." Then Fran enters her house and finds Verna naked on the floor with her clothes spread everywhere.

"Verna, get up and go to bed!"

"I'm in bed now!" Verna quickly responded with an attitude.

"No, you're not! You're on the floor! Looks like you had a good time and a little too much to drink," Fran said sarcastically.

Verna is sleeping and snoring and Fran left her right there on the floor. Then she put a blanket over her Naked Ass and went into the kitchen only to slip on Verna's vomit and landed on her back. It scared Fran more than it hurt her.

"Verna!" she yelled, "no more alcohol for you!" Then she got up with a sharp pain in her back.

Fran was angry as she grabbed a picture of ice water and went to pour it on Verna. First, she snatched the blanket off her and then proceeded to pour the ice water on Verna's face. Verna quickly got up as the cold water shocked her sober.

"Now that you're up, put some clothes on your Naked Ass and clean this water up! Then get that Damn vomit off my kitchen floor! I almost broke my neck!" I should sue your Ass! Oh, I forgot, you don't have any money."

"I'm sorry Fran," Verna said.

"Alright, good night. No sleeping on the furniture or on the floor."

Verna cleaned up the mess and then went to bed, only to wake up with a banging hangover. *And then she said to herself she would never drink again.* Verna learned that she didn't want to live as a sex object as she did in the past; using drugs and alcohol being a shell of a woman.

Her beauty is her only attribute which she used to get what she wanted. She had no lines or wrinkles, no scars or blemishes that you can see. They're all under her skin and in her heart.

Now that she is free, she will fall back into the normal of being female. Because many women go through great lengths to change their faces and bodies. Also, women are conditioned to view their face as a mask and their body as an object. It would become more important to them than the real person they are. Some women don't expect men to be that good looking, but men expect women to be perfect and sexy. But Verna will find her place.

LESSON 30

It's Never Too Late
To Be What You Might Have Been

Tony was steaming mad that Turk got them robbed by someone that they didn't know. A true lesson dealing with people that you don't have a history with. And that the drug trade was full of snakes and scorpions waiting for a victim to come into their line of fire.

"Damn Man! You were pretty Stupid to put us out there like that!" Tony said.

"I didn't know he was going to do that," Turk responded.

"No Shit!" Tony snapped at the Turkish man.

"I'm in the hole for $100,000. And I don't blame him, I blame you! And you owe me $50,000. I'll take two extra Kilos and when you sell them, just give me my money along with the rest of the Shit and we're straight! After that, I'm done with this Shit before you get me killed. Besides, I have a wife and kid at home."

"I want to get home to my wife too," said Turk, "I don't want to get killed either."

Tony immediately responded, "Like I said, I'm done with this!"

Turk then told Tony they had another buyer and he wanted all 9 Kilos for $225,000; $75,000 for Turk and $150,000 for Tony. So, he set the drug deal up with these guys called The Brick Layers. They bought and sold cocaine; they only invested in the best product. If someone sold them some bad stuff, they would not live to do it to anyone else. Because they kill for fun. And if you cross them, they would kill you and everyone close to you.

Turk learned from his last drug deal to set the terms of the meeting place.

The man agreed to meet at a hotel downtown. Tony told Turk that he would shoot him if they got robbed again.

"I…I…I won't get robbed again," Turk said.

"I hope not," said Tony handing Turk the gun that he would use to protect them.

So, the men came in the room and gave it a good search. They looked in the closets, the bathroom, and under the bed. One of the men said that he wanted to check for wires or bugs because he did not trust anyone, not even his own partner. They finally sat down to do business. The men then tasted the Coke.

"This is good!" said one of the men, "if the rest of this Shit is not right, I will find you two, cut your Balls off and feed them to the Rats. I promise you that! Here's your money." The men made the trade and they left.

Tony and Turk got their share of the money. Then Turk pulled out his gun and pointed it at Tony.

"I told you I would not get robbed again. But I didn't say you! Now put the Fucking money in the bag. And maybe you'll get a chance to see your son again," Turk said.

"Just tell me why you're doing this to me?" Tony asked him.

"Because I can," Turk responded, "and you know what? You made a mistake."

"And what was that?" Tony asked looking disappointed and hurt.

"You trusted me and now you're Fucked! So, who's the Stupid one now? So, toss me the money," said Turk still pointing the gun at the regretful man. He did toss the money with reluctance.

"Thank you," he said, "it was nice doing business with you," said Turk.

"Let me have something," Tony pleaded.

Turk said, "You made some money; besides your Daddy got your back. You don't want this dirty money anyway." Then Turk went in the bag that Tony gave him and pulled out a stack of hundreds and threw it at him.

"What's this?" Tony asked.

"It's more that you had a second ago," Turk answered, "I have a plane to catch. I owe some debts back home." And then he looked Tony straight in the eyes, "Are you done with this drug game? If not, you should be."

"You played me!" Tony Yelled.

"I sure did," said Turk, "game over, I win." And Turk opened the door and walked out. And then yelled, "Don't try and follow me!"

Tony sat back in the soft cushion chair in the hotel room angry beyond comprehension and with revenge on his mind.

"I will get my redemption," he said to himself as he sipped on a glass of Royal Crown Cognac.

As he took in the flavor and taste of this fine brandy, he then took in a deep breath and said, "Well, you win some and you lose some."

Tony lost the money, but he gained an experience that he can take with him on his journey through life and sound wisdom, which is worth more than silver and gold. Tony must have the knowledge and the compacity to make use of it. Because if without it, it's like driving down a dark street without headlights and you are sure to wreck something.

Tony picked up is pride, dusted himself off and moved away from his pity pot saying, "Life goes on." He walked to the door and went his way.

Clarissa and Bill got married on June 30, 1988 in a small church on the west side of town. The Bride was beautiful and the groom will have a wife

20 years younger than him. Bill was now 50 years old, a man born into money.

A lot of people attended the wedding; Tony and Jennifer, Fran, Jake Swells, Verna and Bill's other son by his ex-housemaid Nancy Lopez. Bill still supports Nancy by sending her $2,000 a month and sometimes more. The guest are now starting to arrive at the wedding reception.

Fran spoke to Clarissa, "Congratulations."

"Thank you," she replied, "I'm glad you came."

"I would want to miss this for the world," said Fran.

Then Clarissa said, "I have what you can't have and I do what you can't do. I haven't forgotten about our little spat that we had at your former jail home."

"Oh, you're so lucky it's your wedding day or I would beat that pretty gown off your Ass!" Fran said to Clarissa looking straight into her eyes.

"I don't care what you do, just as long as you don't scratch me with your infected nails." Fran rolled her eyes and walked away to keep from making a scene.

"That's right, walk away. Do what you do best," Clarissa said calmly almost under her breath.

Fran walked over to Bill. "Hello Fran."

She shook her head at him, "Are you happy now? I must still like you a little because I didn't knock your wife's teeth out for disrespecting me. Besides, I would not want to mess up this special day."

"Thank you for not acting a Fool," said Bill.

"Your welcome. But next time, she won't be that lucky. I want you to meet someone." Fran waved Jake over; he came to where they were standing.

"Bill, this is my friend Jake," said Fran.

"I think we've met," Jake said looking at Bill, "it's nice to see you again."

"Same here," said Bill, "I will leave you two to chat, my wife is calling me. Enjoy yourselves, eat and drink all you want." Then he slipped through the crowd to meet his wife.

Tony told his father his wife was beautiful and could he trade Jennifer for her.

"No way! She is something special, I wouldn't trade her for the world."

"I'm happy for you," Tony said.

"Thank you, Son."

"Dad, I wanted to talk to you concerning a business I wanted to start."

"How much do you need?" Bill asked.

"About $50,000," he answered.

"Call me Monday and I'll see what I can do."

"Sure thing," Tony said.

"Call me Son, I have to go find my wife. I'll talk to you later." Bill went up to Clarissa to hug and kiss her.

She looked into his eyes and said, "Your ex-wife is a real Bitch. Tell her to stay away from me with her Contagious Ass. I don't want what she has."

"I want you two to be friends," Bill responded.

"I don't like her, she spit in my face. I don't have to deal with her, you do."

The wedding reception was nice and ended with the couple being lifted off in a helicopter. They went to the airport to board their private jet, which they took them to their honeymoon destination.

Fran went home happy and free to love for a second time. The man who would be like a beacon of light on a dark shore to safely bring her in. Fran learned no matter what you go through in life, never give up. And no matter how bad it hurts, keep moving. She also learned that friends and family will keep you when others let you down. And when you treat people good who have done you wrong, they can't stand with you because it makes them uneasy and they flee. Fran eventually married Jake Swells and they lived happily ever after.

Bill Freeman and his new wife Clarissa sat on a beach somewhere in South America enjoying the sun. He once roamed the jungles of Vietnam. But made it out alive only to be scarred by this war and its devices of death. Many people lost their lives making the ultimate sacrifice. Bill wanted to change his life for the better. Sometimes it comes when we least expect it, like a mighty wind or unpredictable situations that sweep us away like an out of control fire. Sometimes change threatens to devour us. The only thing constant is the certainty of change. For that reason, we must adapt or we die. It may be the maxim which all living creatures exist.

Bill finished his honeymoon to return to a new life. He vowed that he would live the best that he could because tomorrow is not promised. He would live each day as if it was his last.

ABOUT THE AUTHOR

The author, Marvin Grayson resides in Wilmington, Delaware and has a creative mind and unique sense of humor. And you will find his gift in his writing.

Marvin uses his time writing in hopes that others will be inspired. Also, he wants them to know that the chapters of their lives are still being written. And it's not too late to become what you've dreamed of.

This book points out that life is full of Lessons and that we must Learn from them.

FINAL THOUGHT

Some LEARN **Early;**

Some LEARN **Late**

And Some **NEVER LEARN!**

Choose Wisely;

YOUR LIFE DEPENDS ON IT!!!